“When I was
to watch the
do it for hour
confessed.

“Well, with any luck that won’t be happening tonight,” Chris told her. “And even if it does go on raining hard, the inside of my truck is pretty waterproof.”

Roe’s eyebrows drew together as she scrutinized him. She wasn’t sure what he was trying to tell her. “Is that your way of saying that you’re ready to take your leave?”

“No, that wasn’t my intention,” he told her. “But I just didn’t want to overstay my welcome,” he admitted.

Where had he gotten that idea? “That isn’t about to happen for a very long while.”

“Oh, good. That means that I get to hang out with your dogs some more,” he told her, tongue-in-cheek.

“My dogs and me,” she corrected the rancher. “Unless this,” she said, moving her hand around in a circle to include just Chris and her pets, “is intended to be a private party.”

He looked at her for several seconds, and then humor began to play on his lips. “It’s whatever you want it to be,” he told her.

Dearest Reader,

So here we are again, at the end of not just another book but at the end of a trilogy. The three baby girls came into the world one very sad, stormy night as their mother followed their late father's directions to get to his childhood home. Suddenly, Mike Robertson was no longer an old man just biding his time and waiting to die, but a man with three little granddaughters to help bring up and a daughter-in-law to look after. His life instantly took on brand-new meaning.

As time went on and the girls grew, Mike found himself proud of them for different reasons and in different ways. Raegan became a builder who joined forces with her husband-to-be to help save the town of Forever from the effects of a terrible drought. Riley became a nurse practitioner whose skills helped to save her late best friend's daughter, a four-year-old who coincidentally was also the daughter of the man Riley had secretly fallen in love with. And as for Rosemary, whom everyone had always referred to as Roe, she became that most necessary of beings in a town full of cattle and horses. She became a veterinarian.

Come watch how her romance grows and develops with the cute rancher she had fallen in love with in high school.

And stay tuned for the biggest surprise of all.

As always, I thank you for giving me your time and reading one of my books (or in this case, three of them). And from the bottom of my heart, I wish you someone to love who loves you back.

All the best,

Marie Ferrarella

Matchmaker on the Ranch

MARIE FERRARELLA

ISBN-13: 978-1-335-59417-4

Matchmaker on the Ranch

For questions and comments about the quality of this book, please contact us at CustomerService@Harlequin.com.

Harlequin Enterprises ULC
22 Adelaide St. West, 41st Floor
Toronto, Ontario M5H 4E3, Canada
www.Harlequin.com

Printed in U.S.A.

USA TODAY bestselling and RITA® Award–winning author **Marie Ferrarella** has written over three hundred books for Harlequin, some under the name Marie Nicole. Her romances are beloved by fans worldwide. Visit her website, marieferrarella.com.

Books by Marie Ferrarella

Harlequin Special Edition

Forever, Texas

The Cowboy's Lesson in Love
The Lawman's Romance Lesson
Her Right-Hand Cowboy
Secrets of Forever
The Best Man in Texas
A Ranch to Come Home To
Meeting His Secret Daughter
Matchmaker on the Ranch

Furever Yours

More Than a Temporary Family

Matchmaking Mamas

Coming Home for Christmas
Dr. Forget-Me-Not
Twice a Hero, Always Her Man
Meant to Be Mine
A Second Chance for the Single Dad
Christmastime Courtship
An Engagement for Two
Adding Up to Family
Bridesmaid for Hire
Coming to a Crossroads
The Late Bloomer's Road to Love

Visit the Author Profile page at Harlequin.com for more titles.

To

Autumn Marceline Ferrarella

Who Brings Sunshine

Into

Our Hearts

And

Our Lives

Chapter One

Yesterday had been one of those extremely long days for Rosemary Robertson. She was affectionately known to her family and friends as "Roe," as well as the "youngest triplet" to her sisters because she had been the last one of the trio to make her appearance that fateful evening that her widowed mother had given birth.

Now, exhausted beyond words, Roe had no recollection of even climbing into her bed. One minute she was making her way into her small bedroom, the next minute she had made contact with her pillow.

She was sound asleep probably before her head had hit her pillow.

She didn't even remember lying down. The one thing she knew was that she certainly hadn't bothered getting undressed. The allure of the double bed had seductively called to her, and the next thing she knew was sleep. It was a good thing that her two dogs, Kingston and Lucy, had stayed on the floor; otherwise, she could have very well flattened one of them, if not both, as her body made contact with the bed.

But after living with their mistress for a number of years, the Bichon Frisé and the petite German shepherd had developed survival instincts when it came to being around the town's veterinarian.

The dogs had also developed certain habits when it came to living with their mistress.

One of these habits involved waking her up at a certain time in the morning. The way her dogs went about this was to lick her face—vigorously—until she would finally open her eyes and respond to them.

And that was exactly the way Roe woke up the next morning, having her face bathed by pink tongues, one very small tongue, one rather large tongue, both of which were moving madly along her cheeks. She had fallen asleep on her back, and each dog had picked out a side, anointing her until her eyelashes finally began to flicker and then, at long last, opened.

Roe groaned, shifting on the bed. She did her best to attempt to wave the dogs away from her face.

"Oh come on, guys, just give me five more minutes. Please." She sighed deeply and attempted to wave the dogs away again, but their licking only grew more pronounced and frantic. Roe gave up. “Okay, okay, I’m up, I’m up,” she told the dogs, struggling into an upright position.

With another deep sigh, Roe scrubbed her hands over her now very damp face, doing her very best to try to pull herself together.

It was a slow process, but she was getting there.

Finally fully awake, she looked from one dog to the other. “You know, if you don’t change your tunes, I can always find a nice home for you two. What do you think of that?” she asked, attempting to pin the dogs down with a look.

The pets apparently weren’t buying it. Kingston, clearly the leader despite his size, began licking her face again and this time, Roe gave up and just laughed at her pets.

“Okay, okay, I know where this is going. Time for your breakfast,” she told the dogs. “But first you’re going to have to let me get up out of bed.” As if by magic—she had trained the two dogs relentlessly when it came to obedience—Kingston and Lucy retreated from her bed. “That’s better,” she said, praising them.

Roe swung her legs off the bed, searching around with her toes for her shoes. She usually wore boots all day, then pulled them off the moment she walked in the front door and put on her shoes in their place.

Finding her shoes, she slipped into them and then stood up.

"Okay, let's go see about that breakfast," she told the dogs.

Her furry fan club all but hopped around her in a yappy circle, not exactly getting underfoot, but not exactly steering clear of her, either.

Roe made her way into the kitchen and began preparing two bowls of food for the dogs. The bowls each had boiled chicken thighs, a tablespoon of pureed pumpkin sauce, a sprinkling of cheddar cheese scattered on top and just enough dog food to make it an all-around meal for the pets.

Once done, she set the bowls down on the floor and watched the dogs go at it as if they had been starved for days instead of fed midday yesterday when her neighbor had come in to leave dishes for her pets that Roe had prepared.

Roe always got a kick out of the fact that Kingston cleared his bowl much faster than Lucy did, despite their difference in size.

"No picky eaters here," Roe declared happily. They had all but cleared their bowls completely in less time than it had taken her to put the meals together. "Well, I hope you enjoyed that because you're not getting anything more until I get home tonight," she told them as she filled their water bowls. "With any luck, today won't be anything like it was yesterday. I hardly got a chance to take two breaths in succession."

As she spoke, Kingston cocked his head first one way, then the other. The dog she had found stumbling around town one morning eight years ago had become attached to her almost instantly. He'd had a large, fresh gash in his rear right leg at the time. She initially thought she might have to amputate it because it looked as if a serious infection was swiftly spreading through the injured limb.

By working diligently and relentlessly, Roe had managed to save his leg and keep the infection from spreading until she was finally able to eradicate it. But it had been touch and go there for a while.

Initially, she had taken Kingston home to watch over him until he got well. Slowly, eventually, her home became his home.

Permanently.

Lucy had turned up on her doorstep a year and a half after that. If she had ever harbored any doubts about her ability to care for animals, Lucy quickly cured her of them. The frightened dog had been easily won over by her. Roe came to the happy conclusion that she had an affinity not just for caring for animals, but for curing them as well.

She stood for a moment now, just looking at the two dogs that had added so much meaning to her life. Roe could feel her happiness radiating inside of her.

It took effort to draw herself away the pets, but she managed.

The rest of the day was waiting for her to get started.

Roe had just gotten out of the shower and hadn't even had a chance to dry off yet when her cell phone began ringing. She shook her head as, still dripping, she glanced over at the phone she had left on the side of the bathroom sink.

"Looks like it's going to be another wonderful, chockful-of-patients day," Roe murmured to herself.

Grabbing her bathrobe with one hand, she picked up her phone with the other and put it on speaker. She rested it on the sink as she punched her arms through her bathrobe sleeves. She wanted to at least begin the process of absorbing the dampness from her body, not to mention having something on to cover her.

"This is Dr. Robertson," she told the caller. "How can I help you?" Roe asked, leaning over the receiver as she raised her voice to a more audible level.

"You could try picking up your phone when I call," the voice on the other end said.

A lot of people who interacted with them said that not only did the three Robertson sisters look alike, they also sounded alike as well.

But those who *really* knew the sisters claimed that they could actually tell their voices apart.

"I was in the shower, Riley. What's up?" Roe asked as she quickly toweled her hair dry with one hand. "And although I know I don't have to tell you this, talk fast. I have an early morning appointment with a rancher."

"Hmm. Business or pleasure?" Riley asked. Roe caught the interested note in her sister's voice, but that could just be because Riley was getting married and she was interested in everyone's situation.

Kingston was watching attentively as Roe swiftly finished drying herself off, then stripped off the now-soggy bathrobe.

"Both," Roe answered her sister matter-of-factly. "My business always gives me pleasure."

"Nice to hear. And how do you feel about weddings?" Riley asked her, deliberately sounding vague.

Roe closed her eyes as she hit her forehead with the flat of her hand. "Oh God, the rehearsal. I forgot all about the rehearsal," she cried. She was supposed to be there later today, after her appointment. "I am so sorry."

"Well, despite the fact that I have a spare sister I can always turn to, I do forgive you. But only because I am so very magnanimous and kindhearted," Riley told Roe. "And it's not like you haven't been to a wedding before and have no idea what to expect or do," she added. And then Riley changed her tone as concern entered her voice. "You sound really tired, Roe. Is everything all right on your end?"

"Honestly?" Roe asked, momentarily at a loss.

"No, lie to me," Riley answered cryptically. "Of course, honestly."

Roe sighed, thinking of the possible threat that might lay ahead when it came to the cattle ranch she had been to the other day. "I'm not sure yet, but that's not anything for you to concern yourself about." She grinned as she made her way into her bedroom, carrying her phone with her. "You have a wedding to plan and nothing else should matter right now.

"Speaking of which," Roe said, continuing her train of thought as she opened her closet and took out fresh clothes for the day, debating whether to bring a second set with her to change into later. She decided it wouldn't hurt to toss them into the trunk, just in case. "Are you sure you want me to be your maid of honor? People might get confused. Especially since you're going to have Raegan as your matron of honor."

Riley laughed, dismissing her sister's concerns. "Anyone who doesn't know that I have two sisters who are mirror images of me really doesn't concern me because they're relatively strangers," she informed Roe. "Just as long as you and Raegan don't get your roles confused, that's all that counts," Riley teased, then went on to clarify the roles. "You are the maid of honor and Raegan is the matron of honor—and Vikki is the flower girl. She is *really* excited about being part of this wedding. When Matt and I asked her to be flower girl, she told me she wasn't able to take part in her mother's first wedding and she is very happy to be able to be part of this one—which I think is adorable."

"You didn't tell her that there wasn't a wedding, right?" Roe asked her sister. "She's a little young to take all that in."

"Vikki is a lot older than the date on her birth certificate claims," Riley answered loftily. "But Matt and I thought we'd save that little tidbit of information for another time just in case after hearing that,

Vikki comes up with questions that wind up stumping us."

"Wise decision. What time do you want me at the church since I missed the original run-through?" Roe asked, referring to the original rehearsal.

"Father Lawrence gave me a list of possible times. Barring an emergency, how does three o'clock this afternoon sound to you?" Riley asked. "Whatever you pick, I'll call the others and tell them. Nobody else has any conflicts. I already checked."

"Three o'clock is doable—barring an emergency," Roe echoed her sister's words, although it would have to be a really big emergency to prevent her from getting there.

"Then I'll see you at the church at three o'clock—barring an emergency," both women said simultaneously, their voices blending. The conversation ended with a laugh. "Bye, Roe," Riley said just before she hung up.

Roe hit the "red" button to end the call. She listened to make sure the call was over, then sighed as she roused herself.

She didn't have time to stare off into oblivion. She had things to do. Not to mention a cattle herd to check out before she could show up at the local church for rehearsal.

There had been an anthrax scare far up north but with any luck, it was either a false alarm or a scare that wasn't going to work its way down to the area surrounding Forever. She had no idea how the local ranchers would respond to that sort of threat if it actually did materialize.

She fervently hoped she would never have to find out. She was perfectly happy to go through life without ever finding out if she was up to that sort of a large-scale challenge. She thought she was, but she would rather not have her abilities tested. Roe honestly felt she was perfectly fine handling mundane things and remaining unchallenged for the entire course of her career.

Dressed in jeans and a work shirt, as well as a denim jacket, and almost ready to leave, Roe came out into the small living room where Kingston was entertaining himself by chasing Lucy around.

"Try not to destroy the house while I'm gone, guys," she told her pets. "I'll try to get home at a decent hour, but I can't really promise anything. Barring any emergency and if the wedding rehearsal goes off on schedule, I'll be able to feed you on time—but don't hold me to that," she said, addressing her words to the lively, fluffy white dog that was busy spinning around in a wide circle in front of her.

She knew it was Kingston's way of trying to entertain her and getting her to stay.

Kingston made a noise, and it was almost as if he actually understood what she was saying to him.

Roe laughed as she petted one dog and then the other. "Glad we understand one another. I will see you two guys later—and remember, you're supposed to guard the house," she instructed.

Not that there was actually anything to guard against, she thought as she locked the door behind her. Forever, Texas, was part of a dying breed: a small, friendly town where everyone knew almost everyone else and looked out for one another to make sure that nothing happened. It was the very definition of the word "neighborly."

There were some exceptions, of course. After all, this was reality and that meant there were people who preferred to keep to themselves and avoid any sort of unnecessary interaction with anyone. But by and large, those people were mercifully few and far between.

For the most part, everyone in the small town knew everyone else and had known them for a very long time. The ones who hadn't been born in Forever had made a strong effort to become part of the town and blend in, often more than those who had been born here.

Roe checked her watch to see how much time she had before she needed to get to the church. Not showing up once was forgivable. Not showing up twice was another story entirely. And besides which, she did want to take part in this. After all, this was for Riley's wedding and she knew how important this was to all parties concerned.

Pacing herself, she paid visits to several of the local ranches to check on how their cattle were doing. Other than a couple of instances—in one case a calf had gotten tangled up in a section of barbed wire and it took a great deal of careful maneuvering to get the animal's horns uncoupled from the fencing—Roe's visits to the ranches were rather uneventful.

She would have never actually admitted it to anyone except for possibly her grandfather, but it was the wedding rehearsal that had captured the major part of her attention.

Because the last ranch on her list was farther away than the other two, it took her a while to get there. Consequently, the trip back took even longer, despite the fact that she hurried and drove her truck faster than normal. It turned out that she was the last one to arrive at the church anyway.

Riley was looking out the church window and was the first to see her coming.

When the front door opened, she greeted Roe, her brown-haired, brown-eyed mirror image with, "Ah, you're finally here. I was just about to send out the search party to look for you."

"Now you won't have to 'cause she's here," Vikki declared happily, a grin encompassing the red-haired little girl's small, beaming face.

"Yes, I am." Roe made her way over to Vikki. "Hi, Angel. How are you doing?" she asked the little girl who was about to officially become part of their family once Riley married Vikki's father, Matt.

"I'm doing fine," the almost five-year-old answered solemnly, as if the question that had been put to her required deep thought. "How are you doing?" Vikki asked, turning the question back on Roe and looking very proud of herself for the accomplishment.

Roe struggled to keep from laughing out loud, knowing it would probably hurt Vikki's feelings. Her exchanges with the little girl always tickled her. She was rather amazed at how well Vikki had learned to cope with her mother's passing.

"I'm doing just fine, now that I see you here," Roe answered.

Her small, smooth brow furrowed as she tried to understand what Roe was saying to her. "You didn't think I would be here?" Vikki asked.

"Oh, but I did. After all, you're the flower girl. I just meant that I was really very happy to see you," Roe explained.

"Oh." Vikki's freshly arranged red hair bobbed up and down as she nodded. "Well I'm happy to see you, too," she told Roe. "How's Kingston? You didn't bring him with you, did you?"

As she asked, the little girl quickly looked around the church in all the places that the dog would choose to hide.

"No, not this time, honey. He's home keeping Lucy company," Roe told Vikki, thinking that was the most understandable explanation she could tell her. "Lucy gets lonely whenever I leave the house."

Vikki thought that over for a minute. "Maybe I could go over to your house and keep her company."

"That's a lovely idea," Roe agreed, but then quickly added, "We'll see. Right now, they need you here for the ceremony."

"Oh, yeah," Vikki agreed, her expression looking almost solemn.

Father Lawrence chose that moment to walk out from his office and into the church proper. He clapped his hands together as he scanned the small gathering before him. It was composed of just the wedding party, not any of the guests.

"Well, it looks like everyone who is supposed to be here is here now," the tall, fair-haired, blue-eyed priest noted. "Shall we get started? Spoiler alert," he said, as if it was meant to be a side comment. "There are no surprises. This is going to be just like the last ceremony I officiated for you, except that it was for Raegan and Alan," he said with a wink. "This time it'll be for Riley and Matthew."

"And me!" Vikki piped up, excited.

Matt laughed and looked in wonder at the daughter he hadn't even known existed such a short while ago. Now her existence filled his heart in ways he couldn't have even begun to imagine. It wasn't until Riley, Breena's best friend, had written a letter telling him about Vikki. He had come to Forever not really knowing what to expect. He certainly hadn't expected to fall in love twice over.

But he had.

"Most definitely you, buttercup," Matt teased, giving the little girl an affectionate hug.

"I'm not a buttercup," Vikki said, pretending to protest. "I'm a girl."

"Yes, you most definitely are that," Matt agreed.

Then he flushed and looked toward the priest, thinking the man was waiting to get started and he was interrupting. "Sorry, Father."

"No need to apologize." Father Lawrence nodded toward the little girl. "I find this sort of display very heartening. But, in deference to those here who are on a tighter schedule and would like to get things moving along, I do suggest we get started." Father Lawrence looked around the immediate area. "Any objections?"

Mike Robertson laughed and shook his head. "Not from this crowd, Father," he told the priest.

"All right, then let's begin—I promise this will be fast and painless, especially since we've already gone through it once before," the priest said as he smiled at the people standing around hm.

Vikki frowned as she tried to follow what the priest had just said. "No, we didn't," she protested.

"Father Lawrence is talking about when he married your aunt Raegan and your uncle Alan," Roe told Vikki, whispering into the little girl's ear.

Vikki's face lit up as comprehension suddenly filled her. "Oh, now I understand," she said. "Sorry, Father Lawrence."

Vikki didn't understand why everyone in the church was suddenly laughing at what she had just said, but she politely refrained from asking because Father Lawrence seemed to want to move things along.

Chapter Two

Mercifully, Father Lawrence had everyone go through their paces just once. When the wedding rehearsal finally ended, he smiled and said, "Well, that should do it. Nothing left to do, folks, but have the actual wedding take place," he told the small collection of people, his eyes washing over them.

"Can't we do it again, Father?" Vikki asked, her small voice echoing around the church and challenging the growing silence.

Surprised, Matt looked at his daughter. Kids her age liked to be outside and playing, not stuck indoors and being quiet.

"Why would you want to do it again?" he asked. He would have thought she would be bored by now.

For all intents and purposes, she had behaved perfectly and been exceptionally quiet.

Vikki answered the question solemnly, her expression looking like the last word in sincerity.

"'Cause I want to make sure that I do it right. It's important to get it right, isn't it?" she asked, looking from Riley to her father. "This is your wedding and weddings are important," she stressed.

Matt didn't even try not to laugh. Getting down on one knee, he put his arms around the petite little girl and pulled her closer to him. He couldn't believe how lucky he was to have discovered he had a daughter after all this time and that she had turned out to be such a little darling. "Just having you here for the rehearsal is doing it right, sweetheart," he told her.

The puzzled look on Vikki's face testified to the fact that she really didn't understand, but she was not about to question such things in a room full of grown-ups. It was obvious she thought they might laugh at her.

Instead, she merely agreed with what her father had said. "Okay."

That was the moment that Miss Joan, the owner of the town's only diner, chose to breeze into the church. It was apparent by her intense expression that she had timed her entrance.

"Hello, Father," she said, greeting the man she'd known ever since he was a small boy. "All done here?" It was obvious that she thought he was and that she was asking what amounted to a rhetorical question.

"Hello, Miss Joan. Yes, we're all done here," Father Lawrence replied with a wide smile, then decided to compliment the woman. "You timed your entrance quite well, Miss Joan."

She didn't bother denying it. "I do my best," she replied. There was no missing the fact that she was quite pleased with herself. Her hazel eyes swept over the small gathering and she nodded. She saw what she needed to.

"Everyone hungry?" She wasn't expecting anyone to say "No."

"Because if you are," she went on, "there's a wedding rehearsal dinner waiting for all of you at the diner. Just follow your noses." Miss Joan looked amused as she waved her thin hand toward the church's double doors.

The way she worded her invitation, as well as her tone of voice, indicated that not only was everyone welcome to come to the diner, they were actually required to come there. Miss Joan was not accustomed to being turned down or having her invitation ignored, and to everyone's recollection, she really never had been.

Miss Joan was about to turn and walk out of the church when Vikki urgently tugged on the hem of the diner owner's dress. Hazel eyes looked down, pinning the little girl in place.

"Yes?" Miss Joan asked in the same voice she used whenever an adult wanted her attention.

"Will there be ice cream there?" Vikki asked her hopefully.

Miss Joan's expression never changed. "After you eat your dinner, yes, there will be ice cream there."

But Vikki wasn't finished asking questions. "Lots and lots of ice cream?" she asked.

Miss Joan treated the question as if it was actually a serious inquiry. "How much you eat is all up to your father," she told the little girl. And then she fixed Vikki with a look that had been known to make grown men flinch. "But a word to the wise, nobody wants to see you exploding, little girl."

The little girl giggled. "I wouldn't do that," she said, waving away the very idea. "People don't explode if they eat too much.

"Well, I certainly hope not," Miss Joan said. "But you never know. Just remember, if you do explode, then you're going to have to be the one who cleans everything all up." She looked down at Vikki pointedly. "Understand?"

Her eyes met Miss Joan's, and she nodded her head up and down so hard, her red hair bobbed almost frantically now.

"I understand," the little girl echoed in a serious tone.

For one of the few times in her life, Miss Joan actually found herself struggling to keep the corners of her mouth from curving upward. There was no doubt about it, the woman got a huge kick out of the little girl, far more of a kick than she had gotten out of a child in years.

Against all odds, she succeeded in keeping any hint of the smile from her face. Only then did she speak, declaring a single word, "Good," and accompanying the single word with a nod of her head. And then, for good measure, she looked around the small gathering. "All right, everyone, get in your vehicles and come on down to the diner," she instructed.

With that, Miss Joan turned on her stacked heel and walked out of the church.

With a laugh, Roe looked in Matt's direction. "You know," she commented, "I think Miss Joan had to have been a general in her previous life."

Absorbing every word that was being said around her, Vikki's mouth dropped open in total awe. "Really?" she cried, her eyes huge. She looked from Roe to her father, as well as at several other faces. The little girl appeared to be utterly captivated by this newest piece of news.

Riley made no effort to keep from laughing. "I think your aunt Roe is teasing you," she told the little girl.

Hearing the comment, Vikki shook her head. "She's not my aunt yet. She won't be my aunt until after the wedding."

Amazed, Matt was beginning to think that it was going to take the combined efforts of all the adults gathered together in the church at this very moment to stay one crucial step ahead of his bright little girl.

"You're absolutely right," he told his daughter. "Tell me, how did you ever get to be so very smart?"

Vikki never even blinked. "I was born that way," she informed him proudly. "Mama said so."

Riley tilted her head slightly, trying to keep the tears from falling from her eyes. Breena would have been so proud of Vikki. Riley could swear she could hear her late best friend's voice talking to the little girl, patiently teaching her things. Breena never talked to Vikki as if she was a child, treating her instead like an adult waiting to happen.

Turning to look at her, Matt thought he saw the glimmer of tears in Riley's eyes. "Are you all right?" he whispered to the woman he was going to make his wife.

Recovering, Riley got hold of herself and flashed a smile at Matt as she took Vikki's hand in hers. "I'm just fine, Matt."

Roe looked on, feeling more than a little envious. She dearly loved both of her sisters and was very happy that Raegan had found someone to love and that Riley had as well, but there was a part of her that was envious of the fact that both of her sisters had found what amounted to their "other halves" while she felt unattached and in all probability would continue to feel that way for possibly the rest of her life.

Oh well, Roe thought philosophically, she had signed on to do her very best to take care of the animals who came her way and that was turning out very well. That was what she needed to focus on, not on what she didn't have.

She got into her own vehicle at the same time that everyone else was getting into theirs. Roe decided to turn on some music to drown out any sad, interfering thoughts that might wind up distracting her. She turned the volume up high and drove herself over to Miss Joan's diner.

Miss Joan wanted this to be a pre-celebratory party, and Roe wasn't going to allow any sober thoughts to get in her way and bring her down.

This was definitely not the time to feel sorry for myself, Roe silently lectured.

This was about Riley and Matt and the sweet little girl who was officially going to become part of their family once Riley and Matt said "I do." Anything she could do to help that happen was absolutely perfect in her book.

When Roe arrived at Miss Joan's diner, she half expected to see a notice on the door declaring that the diner was closed for a private party. But there was no such notice. Miss Joan was apparently juggling both the rehearsal dinner and her regular customers with both hands. She had a section cordoned off so the wedding party, along with Father Lawrence, who had been included in the invitation, were able to sit together while Miss Joan's regulars still had tables available for coffee and their meals as usual.

Vikki gleefully found herself smack dab in the center of the wedding party's seating arrangement. It was obvious to anyone who looked that the little girl loved being the center of attention. She talked up a storm. Riley and her entire family loved Vikki dearly.

"Smile, Roe," Raegan ordered her sister as she came up to join her. "Otherwise, those furrows in your brow are going to be permanent."

Roe had no idea she had been frowning. She flushed. Then, instead of making up excuses about why she looked that way, Roe told her sister honestly, "I'm just worried."

"Well, that certainly narrows things down," Riley said flippantly. "Look, we just came through a history-changing drought and managed to survive just fine, thanks to some of the precautions that our team made. Everything else just naturally winds up taking second place," Raegan assured her.

Roe knew that Raegan knew what she was talking about. Raegan and her husband, along with several of the men he had brought into the project, were responsible for saving Forever from suffering a really terrible fate, possibly a permanent one. They had managed to build a reservoir and also drill for water, bringing it to the all-but-dried-out area and eventually reviving it.

"Not everything," Roe murmured almost to herself.

Raegan was immediately alert. "Would you care to elaborate?"

Roe realized that her sister had heard her. She most definitely didn't want to elaborate. "I don't want to get ahead of myself," Roe told Raegan.

"Oh no, you don't get to toss out unnerving statements and then retreat as if you hadn't said anything at all. Now out with it, Roe. Is there something we should all be bracing for?" Raegan asked.

Before Roe had a chance to come up with an acceptable answer, Riley leaned over and got into the discussion. "What are we talking about and why does my matron of honor look as if she's just bitten into a sour piece of fruit?"

Roe decided to quickly wave away the question. "Nothing to concern yourself about," she told her sister firmly, flashing a smile at Riley. "I told you, all you're supposed to be focused on is your bridegroom, your adorable imp of a daughter, and the upcoming wedding. Everything else is just everything else."

"You know, I'd really feel a lot better about it if you weren't such a terrible liar," Riley told Roe.

"I'm not lying," Roe told her, trying to look like the absolute soul of innocence. "What I am is exhausted," she emphasized. "I got about twelve minutes of sleep last night and just when I was finally drifting off, I was awakened by two madly moving little tongues washing my cheeks and doing their very best to wake me up. Apparently, they thought it was time for breakfast."

Riley looked at Raegan dubiously. "Do you believe her?" she asked the first triplet to exchange marriage vows.

"I'm not all that sure if we have much of a choice. Our sister can be pretty closed-mouthed when she wants to be," Raegan complained.

Roe had had enough. "Stop interrogating me. This is supposed to be a party," she reminded her sisters. "If you're not careful, Miss Joan is going to come over and start asking questions. And you *know* she's not going to retreat until she's satisfied that she managed to get the truth out of us."

Riley looked up as a shadow was suddenly cast over her. "Speak of the devil," Riley murmured under her breath.

"You're not calling me the devil, are you?" Miss Joan asked Riley, coming up behind the two young women and putting an arm around each one of them with just enough pressure exerted to make them realize she had overheard them.

"Oh no, we wouldn't dream of doing that, Miss Joan. Everyone knows you're the very opposite of the devil," Riley told her solemnly.

Miss Joan gave the bride-to-be a very penetrating look. "You're just afraid that I'm going to make you wash all the dishes on this table once everyone is done eating," the woman quipped.

"I can wash them for you," Vikki piped up, happily volunteering her services. The little girl bobbed her head up and down in assurance as she added, "Mama taught me how."

This time Miss Joan actually did laugh out loud, tickled. "I'll keep you in mind if my dishwasher breaks."

Vikki obviously thought that Miss Joan was talking about a person, not a machine. "Do people break?" she asked, wide-eyed.

"Not usually, little one," Riley told Matt's daughter. She pointed to Vikki's dinner plate. "Eat up so you can have dessert," she coaxed.

Picking up her fork, Vikki did as she was told, applying herself diligently to the contents of her plate and quickly making what was on it disappear.

Before she made her way over to the other guests seated in the diner, Miss Joan paused to bend toward Roe. "Before you leave my establishment, I'd like a word with you, missy," she told her.

Roe felt her stomach tightening. This sounded serious. "About?" she asked Miss Joan, the word all but sticking in her throat.

"You'll find out when the time comes and I tell you, won't you?" Miss Joan asked Roe cheerfully. With that, she turned on her heel and made her way to the other guests at the table and then, to the ones in the diner.

Roe sat and watched the woman go. She was afraid to hazard a guess as to what Miss Joan wanted to talk to her about.

Chapter Three

As it turned out, Roe was destined to wait until everyone included in the wedding party finally walked out of the diner before Miss Joan turned her attention to her.

Coming her way, Miss Joan frowned as she looked at Riley's maid of honor.

"You know, you look like you're waiting for the executioner to come your way and throw the fatal switch, electrocuting you," the diner owner commented. Her eyes met Roe's. "I'm not as scary as all that, am I, girl?"

There was no point in trying to bluff her way through this or denying what the woman had just said, Roe thought. And there was certainly no point in lying to her. Miss Joan had a way of seeing through everything.

Roe's eyes met Miss Joan's. Very briefly, she thought of denying it, and then she admitted, "Sometimes."

Contrary to what she expected, Roe's answer seemed to amuse the woman. Miss Joan allowed a glimmer of a smile to pass over her lips before she finally told Roe why she wanted to see her. "Well, honey, the reason I called you over is because, quite frankly, I was worried about you."

"You were worried about me? Why?" Roe asked, confused. Why would Miss Joan even say something like that? She had absolutely no idea where this was going.

"Yes." Miss Joan circled around to where Roe was seated, looking at her critically. "You look like death warmed over, girl." The diner owner studied her more closely, as if she expected to see the answer to her question in Roe's eyes. "You getting enough sleep?"

The answer was no, but she wasn't about to admit that to the owner of the diner. Instead, Roe gave the woman an indirect answer. "I plan to get some tonight. I'm going straight home from here, feeding the dogs and then crawling into bed." She waited to see if that satisfied the woman.

Miss Joan looked knowingly at the girl she had helped bring into the world. "It might help you get that extra sleep you need if you remembered to close your bedroom door at night."

Roe read between the lines. She had no idea how Miss Joan had guessed that her dogs were responsible for waking her up way too early in the morning. But she had made her peace with the same fact as everyone else did. This was Miss Joan and that meant somehow, the woman always seemed to know everything.

So rather than protest, or agree to the idea that she was going to lock her pets out, Roe merely just agreed. "Sounds like a good idea."

Miss Joan snorted as she looked at the vet knowingly. "But you don't plan on doing it, do you? You do know those dogs aren't going to get insulted if you bar them from your bedroom, especially for your own survival." And then the diner owner shrugged, her thin shoulders moving up and down. "But you do what you feel is best."

Finished with her commentary, Miss Joan leveled a piercing gaze at her. "Now go home, girl," she ordered. "I don't want to hear about you falling asleep behind the wheel of your truck and landing in some ditch when I get up tomorrow morning."

"Yes, ma'am," Roe agreed contritely. She gathered her things together and got up from her seat.

The thing about Miss Joan was that beneath all that surface bluster, she knew the woman actually cared. And that, in the long run, was all that really mattered.

Roe didn't quite remember the drive back to her home, but not for the first time, she was really grateful that she lived in town and not on her grandfather's ranch the way she and her sisters had for all those years growing up. The way she felt right now, Roe knew she might have been in real danger of actually falling asleep behind the wheel the way that Miss Joan worried she might.

Falling into a ditch was another matter, though. There weren't all that many ditches to fall into in and around Forever.

She congratulated herself when she pulled up in front of her house.

The moment Roe unlocked her front door, she was immediately greeted by almost nonstop barking. The dogs, she had long ago concluded, were expressing their joy at having her come home. Kingston was racing around her, creating a fluffy white circle until Roe finally bent down to slow him down and run her hand over his fur to pet him.

As if sensing what was going on, Lucy gave the smaller dog a moment to bond with his mistress, then nosed the little guy out of the way so she could have her turn with her mistress as well.

"Yes, yes, I missed you guys, too," Roe laughed despite herself. As she petted each dogshe said, "But you have to promise to be good tonight She rose then and went into the kitchen.

Opening the refrigerator, she began preparing food for Kingston's and Lucy's evening meal. "I'm going to feed you and then I'm going to bed," she informed the dogs, talking to them as if they were absorbing her every word. "Thanks to you guys and your morning alarm system, Miss Joan commented on the fact that I look like I am dead on my feet." She frowned and shook her head. "You can imagine how well that went over."

Their barking grew louder, as if they were expressing their opinion on that.

Roe placed servings of chicken, a sprinkling of cheese and the all-important spoonful of ground pumpkin in each bowl, then brought the bowls over to their feeding spot.

She was convinced that Kingston was going to sprain a least one paw if not two by dancing around her, salivating madly.

"Miss Joan said I should lock you guys out of my bedroom if I want any peace and quiet, but I'm not going to do that—if you two promise to behave yourselves and be good. Do you?" Roe asked, eyeing her two pets as if she expected an answer from them. She placed the bowls of food on the floor. She turned and went to fill up their water bowls.

The dogs lost no time in scarfing up their dinner. Roe had a feeling that, left to their own devices, the dogs would go on eating until they wound up exploding. She was going to need to keep an eye on them, she decided. She definitely didn't want them overeating.

But that was something she would look into tomorrow, she told herself. Tonight was meant for sleeping—which she was going to do immediately.

Roe fell asleep the moment her head hit the pillow. So fast, in fact, that she didn't even notice the blinking light on her answering machine.

The following morning for once, she woke up herself, without the dogs anointing her cheeks in an effort to rouse her from sleep. She had slept later than usual and felt both grateful and a little bit guilty for leaving the dogs to their own devices like this—but mainly she felt grateful.

She stretched, feeling like an entirely new person from the one she had been yesterday morning. She walked over to the door and opened it, then quickly got back into her bed a hair's breadth ahead of the dogs. Sitting up, she patted the place beside her and was instantly rewarded with not one but two dogs bounding over to sit on either side of her.

Their expressions all but said, "Weren't we good? Aren't you proud of us?"

Roe laughed. "Thanks, guys," she told them. "I really needed that sleep. To show you how grateful I am, I'm going to get your breakfast and put it out *before* I take my shower this morning."

As Roe walked into the kitchen, she saw the landline blinking. Whether it had been doing that last night or someone had called earlier yesterday, she had no way of knowing. She was going to need to hit the "play" button to find out.

But that was for after she prepared breakfast for

the dogs. She quickly did a repeat of last night's meal, then set both bowls down on the floor.

"Eat up, boys and girls. Today feels like it's going to be another busy, long day. I've got several appointments coming into my office, not to mention a maid of honor dress to pick up. You wouldn't know about being a maid of honor, would you?" she asked with a laugh as the dogs paused to cock their heads at her, as if they were waiting for her to elaborate. "Trust me, it's a big deal in the human world," she told them. "Anyway, I'll probably be late coming home tonight so I'll leave you a lot of water to tie you over until I can get back."

Finished with the dogs, Roe stretched and yawned, then went back into the bedroom. She was going to postpone finding out who had left the message on her landline until after she had taken her shower.

But as usual, her curiosity got the better of her.

Hopefully, whatever it was could be quickly handled with a "yes" or "no" answer, she thought. Those were few and far between, but they did exist on occasion, Roe told herself, crossing her fingers.

She pressed the "play" button as she held the receiver to her ear.

Roe knew that her friends had far more sophisticated devices when it came to communication, but she tended to gravitate toward more old-fashioned things. She liked those better. There were times when she felt that the world was moving much too fast for her.

"Dr. Robertson," the deep voice on the other end of the call began, "This is Christopher Parnell. I don't know if you remember me or not, but I think I might need your help."

Remember him? Roe thought, amused by his choice of words. She might not have spoken to him for a number of years, but she certainly remembered him. She vividly remembered him from a time when there was no need to refer to her as "Dr. Robertson."

They had gone to school together, with Chris being a couple years ahead of her. At the time, she had had a giant-sized crush on him.

Actually, if she thought about it, Roe mused, a part of her still did, more or less. More than less, she amended. The very thought of seeing him had her blood rushing rather madly through her veins in anticipation.

She could remember watching him in a rodeo competition one summer. The competition involved his coming in first riding his palomino, Big Jake. He had also taken third place in a bronco-busting event, which she had found even more impressive. Roe could recall him looking absolutely magnificent on the back of that horse, hanging on tightly as the horse did his best to buck him off.

But then Chris had graduated high school and, with everything she had been involved in, Roe had lost track of him. She did remember hearing that he had applied to college and was accepted and she had thought that was that. But the following spring, his father had died. The question of who would take care of the ranch came up, but his older brother, Pete, didn't want to be bothered with it. Pete had other plans for himself. He just wanted to sell his share.

Chris didn't want to see the ranch falling into the wrong hands, or actually into any other hands, so he had scraped together as much money as he could and bought his brother out. What he wasn't able to come up with, he borrowed and made arrangements to make regular payments on the property, which he did, although it wasn't easy, until it finally became his free and clear.

She knew all this and admired it. She admired other things about Chris as well, she thought, smiling to herself.

Roe listened to the rest of the message on the machine. The Chris Parnell she recalled from high school had been a happy, fun-loving guy. The voice on her answering machine sounded as if all the fun had been summarily drained out of him.

All he had said was he thought he might have a problem, adding that he never thought he would ever wind up calling her for help. Yet, that was exactly what he was now doing.

He left his number and asked her to call him back at the first chance she had.

Roe really wished she had seen his message earlier, but there was no going back to rectify that error, she thought. All she could do was move forward and do things in the present.

She replayed the message, listening more closely and jotting down his phone number. Roe planned on calling Chris the moment she finished showering and getting dressed.

Fifteen minutes later, she was dried off and dressed and dialing the number she had jotted down.

Instead of getting him, she found she was listening to a recording.

"This is Chris Parnell. I can't answer my phone right now. Leave me your name, your number and a message and I'll get back to you as soon as I can. I'll be branding my cattle in the north forty, so it might be a while before I can get back to you."

The call abruptly ended.

Roe frowned at the receiver in her hand. She really didn't have time to play phone tag, she thought, hanging up the landline receiver. She supposed she could try calling him again later, but this "phone tag" could very well go on indefinitely, and there was something in his voice that made her think he was really worried. She wondered if there was a problem with his cattle.

She remembered him as a far more upbeat guy and not a worrier. Things had obviously changed.

She caught the bottom of her lip between her teeth, and worked it, thinking. He said he was going to be branding cattle in the north forty. She was basically familiar with where that was on his property.

Never one to put things off, Roe decided she could

easily ride over to his ranch to see him and get to the bottom of whatever was bothering him. She had to admit that her curiosity was definitely aroused.

Grateful that there was no wedding rehearsal scheduled for today, Roe finished getting dressed. She pulled on her boots and took off the moment she was ready. She made a mental note on the way over, to call the animal owners who had appointments in her office today and push those appointments up by an hour or so, citing a medical emergency that required her attention.

She smiled to herself. It occurred to her that the people of Forever were basically a very understanding lot. Thank goodness for that.

Chapter Four

Roe was seriously beginning to doubt the wisdom of coming out to the Parnell ranch without making prior arrangements with Chris about exactly where to meet him. She had been driving around for a while now and was just about to give up, turn her truck around and go back the way she had come when she finally saw the rancher on the horizon.

Chris was riding up ahead with a few of his men, trying to corral several heads of cattle. It appeared as if he was attempting to separate the cattle from the rest of the herd.

Roe paused for a moment, taking in the full scene and watching the rancher.

She admittedly was having trouble drawing her eyes away. Chris was riding his palomino and it was almost as if he and the stallion were one entity. Watching him, she couldn't get over the impression that he had created.

It was even more of an impressive figure than the one he had created when he was younger.

The word "magnificent" seemed to be echoing in Roe's brain.

Chris had been good looking when he was younger. But the way he looked now, with his rugged features, brawny shoulders and smiling eyes made him a whole new level of overwhelming and handsome.

Some people, Roe couldn't help thinking, had a way of just getting better and better as they grew older.

Taking her foot off the brake, she began to drive her truck in his direction, cutting the distance between them rather quickly.

"Hey, boss," Jordan Sinclair suddenly spoke up, trying to get Chris's attention. "Don't look now, but it looks like you've got company and she's heading hell-bent-for-leather this way."

"That's not company," Stewart Adams corrected the other wrangler. "That's the animal doc. Dr. Robertson." Adams looked at his boss. "So you *do* think there's a problem with some of the cattle," the wrangler concluded, referring to a conversation he and Jordan had had with Chris earlier in the week.

Chris shrugged as he watched the woman he recalled having gone to school with approaching them in her white truck.

"What I think," he told the two wranglers who were with him, "is that it's always better to be safe than sorry. Always," he underscored.

He was about to turn his horse around and ride straight toward her, but it looked to him as if she had stepped on the gas again and her vehicle had picked up speed.

Chris decided to hold off and wait until she had reached him.

The moment the veterinarian brought her truck to a full stop, Chris got off his horse and, holding onto the mare's reins, he made his way over to her. Without bothering to exchange a greeting or make any sort of small talk, Chris immediately gave in to his curiosity and asked, "What are you doing here?" before she even got out of the truck.

And hello to you, too, Roe thought.

"You left a message on my phone saying you needed to get in touch with me. You made it sound rather urgent, so I decided to come out to your ranch—and here I am," she concluded.

Chris Parnell frowned ever so slightly. "I didn't mean to make you go out of your way like that," he told her. "You should have called."

"I did," Roe told him. "Your answering machine and I had a lovely conversation that led absolutely nowhere because you never picked up or called back. I thought that since this was the first time to my recollection that you actually called, asking for my help, it had to be something important.

"When I couldn't reach you, I moved up all of my other appointments for today and came out to see you." She smiled at him wryly. "Kind of like Mohammed coming out to the mountain instead of the other way around." Taking a breath, she said, "Now that we've gotten that out of the way, why don't you tell me what you think seems to be the problem?" she asked as she got out of the truck.

Closing the door, she looked up at the rancher, trying not to let her thoughts run away with her. "You weren't exactly forthcoming in that message you left," she pointed out, waiting for him to enlighten her.

Chris got right to the point. "Well, in very broad terms, I think there might be something wrong with some of my cattle," he told her as he gestured toward the pasture where they were grazing.

"Could you be a little more specific?" she asked, then said, "The words 'something wrong' encompasses an awful lot of territory. What makes you think there's something wrong with some of your cattle—I take it that you think only some of the cattle are affected," she clarified, watching his expression.

Chris nodded in response to her question. "I've noticed that some of them have become really lethargic," he explained. "In addition, some of them have displayed a loss of appetite and when we try to make them get some sort of exercise, even if it's just moving around a little, they don't. For cattle, they seem to be relatively inert and resist moving around. Now, is it just the weather making this happen—I mean, it has been hot," he asked. "Or is there another reason behind all this happening?"

Roe was already approaching one of the cows that the rancher had indicated. "You mean like this one?" she asked, running her hand along the cow's nose.

Chris nodded. "She would be one of them, yes," he agreed.

Roe slipped on a pair of rubber gloves then began to circle around the animal in question. She looked at the cow closely, then, as she spoke soothingly to the animal, she slowly and carefully checked out the inside of the cow's ears, first one, then the other. Finished, she made her way to the cow's tail, which did not please the animal, but Roe was gentle enough not to agitate the cow. Checking the cow's tail out, she then worked her way over to the cow's underside.

Chris held his tongue for as long as he could, and then he finally asked, "Just what is it you're looking for?"

During the entire exam, Roe was talking to the young cow in a gentle, soothing voice. Right now she was checking out the animal's gums.

"That's what I thought," she said to herself. Glancing over toward Chris, she told him, "Her gums are a pale yellow."

"And what do pale yellow gums mean?" the rancher

asked. He wasn't up on all the different diseases that could strike a cow.

Stepping back, Roe said, "It looks like some of your cows might have a form of anemia." Anticipating his next question, she told him, "It's caused by bush ticks."

He surprised her by saying, "I know what it's caused by. Are you sure that's what's going on here?" he pressed.

"Well, we're going to need to take a blood sample to make sure that's what it is," she told him.

Stunned by the diagnosis, the rancher shook his head in disbelief as he attempted to absorb the information. In all the years that his father ran their ranch, to the best of Chris's knowledge, there had never been a case of anemia to strike the herd.

"All right, so how do we get rid of it?" he asked. "Is there some kind of medicine we can give them, or…?" his voice trailed off.

"Well, the first thing I'm going to have to do once we determine that it *is* anemia is give the cow or cows that have it a blood transfusion so we can get the infection out of their system. If we don't, the infected cows will definitely die. While we're giving them the transfusion, we also need to make sure that they are consuming high-quality feed.

"And once we're satisfied that this infection is out of their system, the cattle will still have to be examined on a regular basis. We're also going to need to make sure the area where they graze is treated with pesticides because we have to reduce the number of ticks that are in the area. Otherwise, we'll be back to square one in no time."

The rancher sighed and shook his head, trying to get his equilibrium back. "I'm beginning to think that my brother had the right idea, selling out and leaving the ranch so that someone else can deal with all of these problems."

She glanced at him. He wasn't fooling her. "Oh, ranching is in your blood and you know it," she told him.

"I'm not so sure about that," Chris replied. He sighed and braced himself. Time to get this out of the way, he thought. "Okay, so how much is all this going to cost me?" he asked her.

"We'll work something out," she promised the rancher. She had a feeling that he was rather low on money and told him, "I didn't get into this for the money."

"Neither did I," he told her, disheartened as he gestured toward his cattle. "But I wasn't looking to starve to death ranching, either."

Roe laughed at the dramatic statement. "Don't worry, you won't. Who knows, I might be wrong," Roe told him in what she hoped was a comforting, reassuring voice.

"And when was the last time that happened?" Chris asked. "You being wrong," he elaborated when she looked at him quizzically.

"Possibly soon," she answered flippantly. "Okay,

first step is to get samples from what appear to be the affected cattle so it can be tested. After all, this just might be a tempest in a teapot."

He looked at her in surprise. "I haven't heard that old saying since I was in Miss Tane's class," he commented, mentioning the name of an English teacher he'd had in high school.

Roe had had the same teacher two years later. The familiar name made her smile. This gave them something in common. "When this is all over, maybe I'll pay her a visit," Roe said.

She headed to the back of her truck and took out a black bag that, among other things, was filled with empty, clear vials she intended to use in order to take samples of the possibly infected blood.

She opened it and then looked at Chris and his two wranglers.

"I'm going to need a hand here, boys," she told them. "I don't have to tell you that these girls are not going to take being poked at and having their blood drawn happily."

All three men nodded, agreeing to help. "Tell us where you want us," Chris said, ready to do what he needed to do in order to help.

"Well, since there's only one of me, we'll focus on just one of the cattle at a time." She looked at Chris. "Pick your favorite and we'll begin there," she told him.

He pointed to the smallest one. "Do Pistachio first," he told Roe.

"Pistachio," she repeated in amusement. "That is a really odd name for a cow," she couldn't help commenting to him.

"There's a reason for that. She looked a little green around the gills when she was born," he told Roe. "I'm a little partial to her because she was the first one whose birth I assisted in after my father died." He grinned more to himself than at Roe. "I almost called her 'Seth' after my dad, but since she was a female, it just didn't seem right to me."

"These days there are a variety of names that can be used, whether the animal—or even the person—is male or female. 'Seth' would have been just as good as 'Pistachio,'" she told him with a wide grin. "Okay, hold Pistachio. If she winds up kicking me, taking these samples might have to be put on hold," Roe told the three men.

With that she took her syringe and very carefully drew a sample of the cow's blood. Finished, she carefully capped off the top of the vial and then went on to label it. She indicated which cow it belonged to, as well as the time and date the sample was drawn.

Placing the sealed vial into her bag, she said, "Okay, let's do the next one."

They proceeded to do Rachel, then Beth, Sadie, Shirley and Ruby.

Roe made sure that each vial was properly labeled and sealed before turning her attention to the next one. All in all there were ten vials filled and labeled by the time she was finished drawing all the blood.

"Is that all of them?" she asked Chris.

He nodded. "As far as I know." He turned to the two wranglers working with them. "How about you? Do you think we should include any more of the other cows?"

"No, that should be all of the possibly infected ones," Jordan told his boss.

Chris turned back to the animal vet—he was still having trouble thinking of her that way, although he was glad she had become one. "You heard them," he told Roe.

She gathered up her black bag, checking the contents one last time and then placed the bag into the truck. "I'll get started on this as soon as I get back into town."

Chris felt guilty having unceremoniously dragged her out to his ranch. "Roe, can I offer you something to eat?" he asked.

But she shook her head. "No, I'm fine. Besides, I've got appointments I've put off, not to mention another wedding rehearsal tonight. I'll grab something to eat later."

"Wedding rehearsal," Chris echoed. This was the first he had heard of that. "Are you getting married?" he asked, staring at her in surprise. A hollow feeling suddenly hit him and he had no idea why.

"No, not me," she told him quickly. "It's my sister Riley—she's the nurse practitioner," she elaborated, attempting to help him tell her apart from her sisters. She knew that had never exactly been a priority for him. Chris had had his own set of friends back in the years that they attended high school.

"Oh," he said. His tone of voice told Roe that at this point, the rancher still had no real way of telling her apart from her two sisters. And right now, it didn't matter as long as she could help his cattle recover. Later, if there was a "later," he could deal with the other minor details.

Chapter Five

Roe was about to finally get into her truck so she could bring the samples to the local lab when an idea suddenly occurred to her. Quite honestly, she had no idea what possessed her, but before she could stop herself, Roe turned toward the rancher.

"If you're not doing anything later on tonight, say around seven, would you like to drop by the church and witness the final wedding rehearsal? You won't have to rehearse," she assured him quickly. "You can just watch it. If I remember correctly, you were friends with Raegan's husband, Alan." Then, in case he was having trouble remembering, she gave his memory a nudge. "He used to come out to Forever every summer until he went off to college. He'd hang out with his cousins, Garrett and Jackson," she prompted, waiting for some sign of recognition to enter Chris's eyes.

"Oh yeah, I remember. He's the one who came to Forever with some of his engineering friends and helped save the town." Chris looked at her. "You had something to do with that, didn't you?"

"Actually, it was my sister Raegan who wound up working with him, not me," she politely corrected the rancher.

Chris shook his head, clearly confused because he had managed to mix the sisters up. "You know, you and your sisters really should wear name tags or different wrist bands so the rest of us can tell you apart."

Roe honestly didn't think that name tags or wrist bands were the solution. "Maybe if you saw all three of us in action, that might help you be able to tell the difference between us."

It had been a while since he had seen them but as he remembered it, all three were completely and totally identical. But he was willing to admit that he was wrong—*if* that was actually the case.

"*Are* there differences between you?" Chris asked, somewhat intrigued.

"Oh, most definitely," Roe assured him, the corners of her mouth curving. "I'm the kind one," she told him with an amused glimmer in her eyes. And then Roe became serious again. "So how about it? Would you like to get away from ranch life and all its problems for a few hours?"

And then it suddenly occurred to her that, for all

she knew, he might be seeing someone and she was butting in where she absolutely did not belong. "Or am I treading where I shouldn't be?" she asked him, quickly attempting to back away.

Feeling quite awkward, Roe quickly attempted to extract herself from the conversation before Chris could say anything.

"You know, never mind. You're probably busy." She waved a hand at her previous invitation. "Forget I ever asked anything."

Chris just stared at her, fascinated by this rather unusual, heretofore unknown side of the pretty, perky veterinarian as she swiftly backtracked.

The rancher cocked his head as he continued studying the veterinarian, then caught himself grinning at her.

"I don't remember," Chris confessed. "Did you always argue with yourself this way or is this something new since you became a veterinarian?"

"I'm not arguing with myself," she told him defensively. And then, blowing out a breath, Roe amended her protest. "That is, I'm not exactly arguing with myself. I just didn't want you to feel that I was backing you up against a wall with this invitation. I mean, you do have a choice here," and then she elaborated, "meaning you can come to the church—or not."

Roe caught herself smiling at the concern the rancher displayed when it came to her behavior. She hadn't meant to come across like that. Chris really was every bit as nice as she had recalled him being, she thought.

Initially, she had thought that maybe it was his looks that had gotten to her again. She could remember being extremely attracted to him back in high school—and rather disappointed when he had gone away to attend college.

When Chris had to come back because his father had died unexpectedly, she had moved on with her life. And Chris had gotten caught up in his.

But there was a small part of her, albeit a very small part, that had held out some hope that Chris would eventually re-enter her life in some form or capacity—especially since she had gone on to become a veterinarian and he was running the family ranch.

"So what's the verdict?" she asked Chris, her hand on the key in her truck's ignition, ready to turn it. "Do you want to come to the rehearsal or not?"

"Is this an official invitation?" Christ asked her archly.

Some might have hazarded a guess that she was overstepping her bounds since this was not her own wedding rehearsal, but she couldn't see Riley or Matt finding any fault in her extending the invitation to an "old family friend," which was probably the way that Riley would see Chris.

"Yes," she said to the rancher with finality. "You can most definitely consider this an old-fashioned, 'official' invitation."

"And it's being held at the church?" he asked, attempting to pin down the main detail that he needed to know.

She nodded, growing progressively more pleased with the reaction she was getting.

"Yes, it's at the church. And with any luck, once the rehearsal is over, we'll all head to Miss Joan's diner for a late rehearsal supper, the way we did the last time."

That caught his attention. Ever since his mother had moved on after his father had died and his brother had sold his interest in the ranch, Chris had been preparing his own meals, such as they were. Cooking had never been one of his better accomplishments. Miss Joan, he recalled, had some really great cooks working for her at the diner. He was usually too busy to go into town for a meal, but this really seemed like a perfect excuse.

"Is that what happened after the last rehearsal?" he asked Roe.

She could tell she had managed to get his attention, Roe thought. She smiled at him as she nodded her head.

"Absolutely. So," she raised her brow as she looked at the rancher, "are you in?"

There was no hesitation whatsoever on his part. "Oh yes, I'm in," he replied, then added a coda, "Although I might be late—"

"No problem," she quickly assured him. "You're not in the wedding party, you're just there to celebrate the fact that a wedding is going to be taking place." She flashed him a smile, pleased she was able to come up with a decent excuse to use. "So, I'll see you there," she concluded.

Roe was about to take off when he called after her. "Wait. You still haven't told me how much I owe you," he reminded her.

"I'll let you know when I get these blood samples to the lab," she told him. The results would give her an indication of what the charges would be.

But he was obviously worried about the cost, so he was honest with her. "After buying out my brother, I don't have all that much money these days. I might not be able to pay you back the entire sum right away."

Her eyes met his. "Do I look worried?" she asked, pleased by his thoughtfulness. "Besides, I know where you live." she added with a wink.

Her wink went straight to his gut and he grinned at her, amused by what she'd said. "Yeah, you do. See you tonight."

Roe turned the key in the ignition and her truck came to life. She waved at the rancher. "Tonight," she echoed as she pulled away.

For just a second, she felt her pulse fluttering in response to the look on the rancher's face. But she needed to get her mind back on her work, Roe upbraided herself. The road was wide open and empty, but she knew there was a certain danger in not paying attention to where she was going.

Roe focused on the next call that had been on her list before she had wound up putting Chris at the top of her list.

* * *

Three hours later, she was finished with all the calls that had been on her list for the day. None of the animals required as much attention as Chris's cattle had—and as far as she was concerned, that particular case was still pending.

She turned her truck toward town. Stopping at the lab, she dropped off the samples with the owner's assistant, then drove to her house.

The moment she came through the door, Roe was greeted by Kingston and Lucy, who immediately all but went into a frenzy as they danced around her. Roe allowed herself a few minutes to enjoy the reunion then separated herself from the dogs.

"I know you don't care, but I need to change my clothes before I go to the wedding rehearsal."

For once, she was actually looking forward to the rehearsal. Chris agreeing to swing by the church meant a great deal to her. She knew she shouldn't be building up her hopes, but she just couldn't help herself. This was the first time in a long time that she was actually attracted to someone—the last time, she thought, had been in high school.

And that had been to Chris Parnell as well.

"You guys are in luck this afternoon," she told the dogs as they jumped up and down around her. "I'm feeding you early because there's another rehearsal and since this is the last one before the actual wedding takes place, we're all staying until we get everything right," she said with a hint of amusement.

Going into the kitchen, she took out the usual two bowls and prepared her pets' meals, this time adding a little extra to each bowl.

"Eat slowly," she counseled as she put the bowls down on the floor, then laughed. "Like you guys have a clue what that actually means. But just so you know, when I come home tonight, I won't be feeding you again. The most you can hope for is to get one treat apiece—a small treat."

She paused to fill the water dishes and then went into her bedroom for a quick shower and to change. For once, she closed the door. She didn't want any furry help when she got dressed for the wedding rehearsal.

Moving quickly, she showered, then changed into her maid of honor dress. She gave herself a quick once-over from all angles, then slipped on her shoes.

Finished, Roe opened the door. Both pets were waiting for her right outside her bedroom.

"Pretty, isn't it?" she asked the dogs, looking herself over in the mirror one last time.

Lucy made a whining noise in response as Kingston attempted to check her out. Roe very gently made him back off.

"I want no paw prints or dog saliva on this, at least not until *after* the wedding is over," she warned both of the dogs. "Okay, see you guys later. Be good and guard the house."

It was a short drive to the church. As she drove there, Roe told herself not to get caught up or carried away, but the truth of it was, she needed a break from all her responsibilities as much as Chris seemed to.

With both of her sisters spoken for, she saw a rather solitary life ahead of her, filled with work. She felt she should take her fun where she found it.

With that in mind, she parked her truck and hurried into the church.

"You look like you're up to something," her grandfather said, coming over to her as she entered the building. As usual, she was the last to arrive.

Father Lawrence was about to begin the rehearsal, but he needed to see to something before he began so Mike took that opportunity to talk to his last single granddaughter.

"Did everything go well today?" Mike asked. "Did you manage to fit in and see all your patients?"

Roe nodded her head as she smoothed out the bottom of her dress. "Yes, thanks for asking. I did manage to fit them all in, Pop," she told him. "With the exception of Chris Parnell's cattle, all the problems turned out to be minor ones."

"What about Parnell's cattle?" her grandfather asked, curious.

"I took samples of their blood to see if they have something minor, or if they're suffering from anemia."

"Could they be?" her grandfather asked, concerned. This could turn out to be a major problem.

"I don't know, but the symptoms Chris initially described indicated that might be the case. Anyway, I took the liberty to invite him to the rehearsal," she told her grandfather. "I thought it might distract him for a while. He looked like he needed it. That is okay, isn't it?"

"Why shouldn't it be?" her grandfather asked her. "If you ask me, the poor guy could use a break from his problems."

She flashed a smile at her grandfather. "That's what I thought, too. Glad you agree, Pop."

"You need to trust your gut, girl," Mike Robertson told his last unattached granddaughter. "After all, you trust your gut when it comes to treating the animals. You should extend that to the way you interact with people," he told her, looking at his granddaughter knowingly.

"I haven't the slightest idea what you're trying to infer, Pop," she told the man, feigning innocence.

He eyed her. "Uh-huh. And then there was the one about the three bears," her grandfather said.

Standing a few feet away from them, Vikki's head shot up at the mention of the fairy tale. "I know that one, Pop," she declared proudly. "Want me to tell it to you?" The little girl looked from Mike to Roe, smiling broadly. "I can, you know."

"After we finish with the rehearsal, sweetheart," Mike told her. Roe, he noticed, was looking toward the church's double doors even as Father Lawrence called for everyone to take their places for the final rehearsal run-through.

He smiled knowingly to himself. It wouldn't be long now.

Chapter Six

The wedding rehearsal was close to half over when Roe finally heard the church doors open. Turning in anticipation, she smiled when she saw Chris walking in.

She had to admit that she expected the rancher to be wearing the same outfit she had seen him in earlier in the day. But to her surprise, he had changed out of those clothes and was wearing what appeared to be a light blue dress shirt and a dark, navy blue jacket and matching slacks.

Chris wasn't wearing a tie, but she probably would have become light-headed if he had, Roe thought cryptically. She smiled to herself. The rancher looked really, really handsome. She had to concentrate in order not to sigh.

She saw him slowly scanning the area as he walked

in, and then his eyes met hers. Roe fought a very strong desire to make her way over to him and say something. Anything.

But she knew if she did that, it would definitely be interrupting the wedding rehearsal. She had to keep reminding herself that this wasn't about her. Having Chris here observing created a small sidebar for her in what was going on. But this most definitely was not about her, except perhaps in the most minor of ways.

When the door opened, Father Lawrence turned toward the visitor and nodded a greeting. He knew Chris by sight, but other than the man's father's funeral, the priest had not interacted very much with the rancher.

"Welcome," he said, greeting Chris. "We're almost halfway through. It's going rather well," Father Lawrence told the man, pleased. "With a little bit of luck, we'll be finished before you know it," he promised. "So, if you'll just take a seat in the back of the church," Father Lawrence suggested, waving his hand toward the rear pews.

Chris nodded. He hadn't expected everything to stop on his account anyway. "Sure thing, Father," he said as he made his way toward a pew.

Father Lawrence paused for a moment, as if he was trying to recall who the young man who had just arrived was. He didn't want to take away too much time from the wedding rehearsal he was conducting, but he had to admit that something was nagging at him.

And then it hit him. "Didn't your father die rather unexpectedly a couple of years ago? I remember officiating over his funeral service," Father Lawrence recalled.

Pausing before he slid into the pew, Chris nodded. "He did and you did. You conducting the service meant the world to my mother," he added with feeling. He could still remember the grateful look on his mother's face.

Father Lawrence heard what wasn't being said. "How about you?" he asked, wondering how the rancher was affected by his father's service.

"I have to admit that I was a little too shell-shocked at the time for the service to actually create an impression and sink in," Chris answered honestly.

Father Lawrence nodded. He had heard this sentiment before. "I understand." And then he looked around at the group standing before him. The rehearsal had come to a complete standstill. "Sorry, folks," he apologized. "But we're all friends here, so I'm sure you'll all indulge me with this little sidebar."

"Don't give it a second thought, Father," Rita told the man who would soon say the words that would permanently bind her second daughter, Riley, to a young man Rita had learned to admire greatly. "Feel free to take as much time as you need," she encouraged with a bright smile.

It was the kind of atmosphere Father Lawrence

welcomed, both in his congregation on Sundays and in the ceremonies he found himself performing. Inclining his head, he smiled at the mother of the bride and said, "Thank you." Then, scanning the rest of the group, he went on to say, "All right, people, let's get back to this rehearsal, shall we? I hear that Miss Joan is eagerly waiting to usher you into the diner to feed all of you."

Matt looked at Riley. "Works for me," he told his almost bride with a very broad smile.

"Me, too, Daddy," Vikki eagerly piped up.

Father Lawrence laughed. "Looks like the young lady has spoken," he said to the rest of the wedding party. "So let's get this show on the road." the priest proposed, launching into the final portion of the wedding ceremony.

The wedding rehearsal went quickly and smoothly without a single hitch. Riley and Matt even got through their wedding vows in a single recitation.

Father Lawrence nodded his head and smiled in satisfaction as he closed the missal he was holding in his hand. He had actually committed the ceremony to memory a long time ago, but he still liked holding the missal to help him get through it. It was like a good luck talisman.

"I'd say you are all as ready as you are ever going to be," the priest declared, looking at the happy couple.

Matt laughed. "You'll get no argument from me," he told Father Lawrence.

"Not from me, either," Vikki announced solemnly with a very serious expression on her face.

Unable to help herself, Riley laughed and hugged the little girl to her. No matter the situation, Vikki could always make her laugh.

The wedding participants began to rise and gather their things together as they prepared to leave the church. They were focused on making their way over to Miss Joan's diner.

Roe noticed that Chris was watching everyone as they prepared to leave. It struck her as rather odd that he wasn't moving.

"Aren't you coming to Miss Joan's diner?" she asked the rancher.

Chris turned toward her, a quizzical expression on his face. "I don't know if I'm invited."

Roe's brow furrowed just a little. He was kidding, right? "This is Miss Joan's diner. Of course, you're invited after the wedding rehearsal. Why wouldn't you be?"

He told her the first thing that had occurred to him. "Well, for one thing, I'm not part of the wedding party, nor am I part of the rehearsal," he pointed out.

Roe laughed. "Miss Joan won't hold that against you," she informed him simply. "Besides, you're a friend of the wedding party. That's enough for Miss Joan."

But that wasn't enough to convince the rancher. He waved the animal doctor's words away. "She won't even know that I'm not there."

She looked at him as if he had lost a few marbles. "This is Miss Joan. She knows everything. And," Roe added, "I guarantee that if you don't come after being here, she'll be insulted. I don't care who you are. You do *not* want to insult Miss Joan. Ever."

"You realize that you're making the woman sound like a dragon," he told Roe.

Her expression never changed as she looked at the rancher and deadpanned, "And your point is?"

Chris laughed as, getting her point, he shook his head. "Maybe I've been spending too much time mingling with cattle and not enough time mingling with people."

She hooked her arm through his as she directed him toward the church's double doors and the way out. "Well, let's see if we can fix that, at least for one evening."

He had no idea what possessed him to say, "Fine by me," but he heard himself readily agreeing to go along with her suggestion and partaking of the rehearsal dinner as well.

Chris was rewarded with a huge smile from Roe and, as it had done earlier, it seemed to go straight to his gut. And when it did, it created a warm ripple that seemed to swirl all through him.

Once outside, Roe gestured toward his vehicle. "Do you want to drive over to Miss Joan's diner with me or on your own?" Realizing that there was a third choice available, she added, "Or do you want to go with someone else?"

He looked at her curiously. As far as he knew, there really wasn't anyone available for him to impose on. Ever since he had taken over the family ranch, buying out his brother's share, he had stopped socializing with anyone other than the wranglers who worked for him. There was no time left over for anything else.

Still, curious, he asked her, "Do you have anyone else in mind?"

"Not really," she admitted. "But I thought you might."

Chris shook his head. "Nope," he told her freely.

Roe nodded. "All right, it's settled, then. You're coming with me," she informed him. "My truck is over here," she pointed toward the vehicle. "And after we finish eating at Miss Joan's, I'll bring you back to the church so you can pick up your car. How's that sound?" she asked him, waiting for him to agree.

Chris couldn't help smiling. The woman made him think of a drill sergeant.

Chris walked over to the passenger side door of Roe's truck. Once she unlocked the doors, he got in.

Roe slid in behind the wheel on her side and put her key into the ignition. The truck hummed to life. Getting out of the church parking lot took a few minutes because everyone had to wait their turn as they cued up toward the exit.

Roe glanced in Chris's direction. It occurred to her that he hadn't asked her about the tests that were being performed at the lab.

"I dropped off the vials at the lab. I should have the results by mid-morning tomorrow, if not sooner," she told him.

"So we have to wait until then?" he asked. For some reason, he had thought it would take less time than that.

Roe nodded her head. "I'm afraid so—unless you know of a magical way to get the results faster," she told him.

Chris pressed his lips together, thinking. He had another question for her. "What are the odds in favor of the bloodwork coming back clean?"

"One of the first things my grandfather taught me," she said as she followed another vehicle out of the lot and drove her truck toward Miss Joan's diner, "was don't borrow trouble. If it's there, trouble will find you fast enough. This whole thing is a wait-and-see situation."

Chris's mouth curved ever so slightly as he nodded his head. "I always thought of your grandfather as being a very smart man."

"I'll tell him you said that. The man can never get enough compliments," she told the rancher with a wide smile.

Chris was quiet for a few minutes, thinking. And then he asked her, "So, do you think I have anything to worry about? Seriously."

This was not the time to give him odds and talk about the possible downside of the tests if they come back positive that his cattle have the disease.

"We will handle this," she promised the rancher. "Caught in time, this kind of thing can be erased and you won't wind up losing any of your herd."

"But considering how serious this disease can get, there have been instances involving herds that were lost," he interjected.

"Uh-huh," she responded, listening. "And floods and earthquakes have been known to happen as well—but they don't always happen. For now, just focus on the plus side of things and how they can go."

"That's not always easy," Chris told her in all seriousness.

"Half the battle," Roe told him, "is wanting to focus on the plus side. *Really* wanting to," she emphasized. And then she pointed out, "There's Miss Joan's diner."

Pressing down on the gas pedal, she maneuvered the truck into the diner's parking lot ahead of several of the other vehicles that were coming over from the church. Her eyes on the spot she had picked out, she zipped into it in one smooth movement.

Chris found himself holding onto the arms of his seat in order to stay in it. "Who taught you how to drive?" he asked.

"Pop gave me a couple of my first lessons, and then I just took it from there. Why?" she asked as she got out of the truck, closing the door behind her.

"No reason," he replied innocently, then told her with a broad smile, "I just wanted to know who I should avoid getting into a vehicle with."

"Very funny," she commented, locking the truck.

Leading the way to the diner, she hurried up the stairs to the front door.

"I wasn't trying to be funny," Chris replied quietly, saying the words more to himself than to her.

At the top step, Roe turned around and looked down at Chris. She wasn't sure if she had heard him, or if she had heard someone talking from inside the diner.

"Did you say something?" she asked.

She was his veterinarian and his ride back to the church. He felt it was prudent to keep his cryptic words to himself.

"I didn't say a word," he told her innocently.

Chapter Seven

Miss Joan watched the people she had invited for a meal come filing in. The wedding rehearsal had taken longer than she had anticipated. But she also knew this was the last rehearsal before the big event this Saturday so that anything that needed to be ironed out would be taken care of.

Making her way over to Riley and her fiancé, Miss Joan offered them what passed for a smile.

"So, are you two ready to get married?" the owner of the diner asked the duo, looking at each of them.

It was Vikki who spoke up and answered the woman's question. "You bet we are!" was her enthusiastic response as she beamed at them. "And it's the three of us," the little girl corrected her.

One arm laced around his daughter's shoulders,

Matt hugged the little girl to him. "I guess that says it all for us," he told Miss Joan.

Unaccustomed to holding anything back, Miss Joan looked at the young man with approval. "Well, I have to admit that I did have my doubts about you in the beginning, boy, but I guess you turned out all right after all," she told him with an approving nod.

"He's my daddy," Vikki informed the woman as, putting her hands on her hips, the little girl assumed a defensive stance. "Of course, he's all right." She looked up at Matt. "Right, Daddy?"

Matt smiled down into the small, beaming upturned face. "Right, Angel," he replied.

Vikki's face screwed up just a little as she tried to process his answer. From her expression, it looked as if it didn't seem to make any sense to her. "I'm not an angel yet, Daddy. But maybe someday…" she told him cheerfully.

Miss Joan looked around at the gathering that had come into her diner. "Why don't we table this discussion for now and get some food into you people?"

She didn't expect to be argued with. There was no arguing with the woman.

And then Miss Joan turned toward the food server she had previously briefed regarding the meal. "Lily, show these nice people where they're going to be sitting." Miss Joan waved her hand toward the cluster of tables that had been pushed together for this exact reason to form one large unit. "Although I doubt that they could actually miss that," the diner owner speculated with a veiled laugh.

Miss Joan was surprised when Vikki came up beside her and tucked her small hand into the woman's thin, bony one. Cocking her head to look up at the woman, Vikki requested, "Show me, please."

For a second, Miss Joan smiled broadly down at the little girl, then the diner owner glanced over toward Roe. "Don't think I didn't see you whispering into Vikki's ear, sending her over here," the diner owner said, then added, "I'm not a fool."

Roe's expression was the absolute picture of innocence. "I have no idea what you're talking about, Miss Joan."

Miss Joan laughed at Roe's protest. "Right. Like I was born yesterday," she scoffed.

"No, you weren't," Vikki insisted. "I saw you yesterday. You weren't a baby," the little girl declared. "You were as big as you are now."

No one laughed louder than Mike Robertson at the words that Vikki had blurted out. He turned to look at the diner owner. "She's got you there, Miss Joan."

Miss Joan made a dismissive noise, eyeing the girls' grandfather. "Trust you to point out the obvious, old man." It was time to get these people fed, she thought. "Okay, everybody. Settle down, settle in and place your orders." She turned to the young woman she had selected to collect the information and serve the food. "That's your cue, Lily," she declared just before she turned on her squat heel and made her way back behind the counter.

Roe glanced at Riley and Matt. "Why don't you, Matt and Vikki start us off?" she suggested with a wide smile. "That way, the rest of us can just fall into place right behind you," she told her sister and her wedding party.

Riley leaned over the table toward Chris. The rancher was sitting next to Roe. Since she was about to marry a man she had fallen for ever since Breena had talked about him in such glowing terms, even before her best friend discovered that she was pregnant with his child, she wanted that same exciting, heartwarming turn of events happening to Roe.

Roe, Riley knew, had nursed a crush for the rancher since they were both in high school.

"Don't let her scare you off, Chris," Riley said. "Roe likes being a dictator, but she really doesn't mean anything by it," she told the rancher, grinning at him.

"Unlike Riley," Roe told Chris with finality, "who absolutely *loves* being a dictator. Order something, Riley," she prompted her sister. "That way, when it comes you'll have something to put in your mouth so you can stop talking so much and give the rest of us a little rest."

Mike looked toward the future groom. "You sure you want to marry into this family, boy?" he asked the young man, giving him a penetrating look. "I'd think twice about that commitment if I were you," the girls' grandfather chuckled, amused with himself.

"Pop!" Rita scolded, surprised as well as somewhat dismayed by the warning the older man had given to his future grandson. "He doesn't mean it," she quickly assured Matt. "Nobody dotes on those girls more than my father-in-law does."

Matt laughed. He had been around the family for the last six months and in that time he had bonded with and acclimated to all of them in different ways. He knew exactly what he was getting into—and he really couldn't wait.

"I realize that. Riley's grandfather has more patience and more sterling qualities than my own grandfather ever had," he said to his future mother-in-law in all honesty. "I'm very glad that Vikki and I are marrying into such a happy, well-adjusted family. Nothing brings that home to a person more," he told Rita, "than having kids of your own to consider and to make you see things more clearly."

"Hear that, Roe?" Raegan asked her sister with a wide grin. "This poor man thinks we're well-adjusted. Shows you what a sheltered life he must have led," Matt's future sister-in-law said.

"You *are* well-adjusted," Mike insisted, giving Raegan a penetrating look that all but ordered her to *cease and desist*.

"You're all just a little worn out, that's all. Isn't that right, Raegan?" he asked, giving the young woman who had been born ahead of her two sisters a warning look.

Raegan had always known just when she needed

to back away from a topic. Right now, she flashed a wide, easy smile in her grandfather's direction.

"Whatever you say, Pop. You've always known me a lot better than I've known myself," she told the man in all seriousness, as well as with an abundance of love.

Mike chuckled, pleased by Raegan's remark. "Well, ain't that the truth?" the girls' grandfather acknowledged with a nod of his head. His eyes swept over the members of the wedding party.

Miss Joan picked that exact moment to poke her head in. She looked around at the people who were seated at the large, makeshift "table" that had been pulled together, making a whole out of the various parts. There were no plates of food sitting in front of the wedding party. The owner of the diner frowned deeply as she looked at the participants.

"Feel free to order your dinner any time you'd like. The diner doesn't close up until midnight—or thereabouts," she emphasized with feeling, telling them what they already knew.

Her meaning was clear.

Eat.

Roe leaned forward and addressed Chris in a very quiet voice, "I think that was Miss Joan's not-so-subtle way of telling us to get around to placing our orders and start eating immediately. She doesn't like having her plans—large or small—ignored."

Overhearing Roe, Miss Joan turned around to face her and the rancher. "And if that's too 'subtle' for you, I can always hit you over the head with the menu."

Roe flashed a grin at the owner of the diner. Leave it to Miss Joan, she thought. "Message received, Miss Joan. Loud and clear."

"Good," Miss Joan declared forcefully. Beckoning over a second server, she told the wedding party, "Place your orders, ladies and gentlemen. Annie here will be more than happy to take them for you. Between Annie and Lily, you'll get to eat twice as fast." Turning toward the girls' grandfather, she added, "That includes you, too, old man."

Chris waited until the diner owner had made her way back behind the counter before he asked Roe, "Has she always had such a laser tongue, or is this something that developed over time?"

Roe thought that was a rather strange question for someone who had been born in Forever to ask. "You sound like you didn't come by here very much."

"The truth is, I didn't," Chris admitted with a vague shrug. "My mother thought it was a huge waste of money to come to the diner to get something to eat since she could make me anything I wanted to eat or drink at home," he told Roe. "Or, if she couldn't, she felt that I really didn't need to have it in the first place."

Roe stared at him, finding this information a little difficult to absorb. The diner was as much for socializing as it was for eating. "So you really never came to the diner just to grab a soda and hang around with your friends?"

The rancher shook his head. That was just a foreign concept to him. "Nope. There were too many chores to take care of on the ranch. Between that and doing my homework, there was never any time to just hang out with my friends. Besides, my mother frowned on that sort of 'unproductive' behavior. She thought of it as just being plain lazy."

Chris expected to be on the receiving end of some sort of cryptic comment from the veterinarian. Instead, he saw compassion in her eyes.

"You poor guy," she told him, her voice filled with sympathy. "It sounds like you definitely needed some 'me' time, back then as well as now. What do you do to kick back and enjoy yourself?"

"I sleep. And once in a blue moon," he said with an amused smile, "I let myself be dragged out to observe a wedding rehearsal—topped off with a really good meal."

She felt somewhat sorry for the rancher but refused to be pulled in by that feeling. Chris didn't need her to feel sorry for him, she thought. Instead, she told him, "You're also invited to my sister's wedding, you realize that, right?"

Chris shook his head. "Until right now, no, I didn't realize that," he admitted. He paused for a moment. He didn't want to insult Roe, but he didn't want to assume anything incorrectly, either. "Isn't the wedding invitation really supposed to come from the bride and groom?"

A soft smile curved her mouth. "You might not have noticed this, but my sisters and I are triplets," she told him, tongue-in-cheek. "That means for the most part, the three of us think alike and are usually in complete agreement with one another. That means we agree on who's invited to our various parties—or weddings," she added with a twinkle in her eye.

But the rancher wasn't really completely convinced. "Shouldn't Riley and Matt have the final say when it comes to their guest list?" Chris asked.

"Trust me, they won't find fault in having you attend. If anything, they'd view *not* including you as an accidental oversight." She pointed to the dish that the server had deposited in front of him. "Now, eat your pork ribs before they start getting cold and Miss Joan materializes next to your elbow to comment on how you're wasting precious food."

Chris looked dubiously at the woman beside him at the table and then laughed at the suggestion. "Doesn't Miss Joan have better things to do than police the diner?"

Roe shook her head at the suggestion. "Miss Joan has the ability to be in all places at seemingly the same time. She has her priorities, but she doesn't allow anything to ever slide."

Chris laughed as he shook his head. "You make her sound like she's an omniscient being."

"And your problem with that is—?" Roe wanted

to know. She reached for her knife and fork, her hunger growing in mounting proportions.

"No problem," he answered. "Just trying to get all my facts straight so I can keep them that way. One question," Chris said as he began to eat his dinner.

And then he paused for a moment as a surprised, pleased smile slid over his lips. This was *really good*, he caught himself thinking. A lot better than he would have anticipated it would be.

He realized he had missed out on a lot these last few years by not patronizing the diner.

"Go ahead," Roe urged, waiting for the rancher to ask his question. When he didn't, she prodded, "What is it that you wanted to ask me?"

"Does she walk on water, too?" he asked, amusement shining in his eyes.

"Only when it's raining," Roe told him, maintaining a straight face even as the corners of her mouth were struggling not to curve. "And at times," the veterinarian continued, "not even then."

Her eyes were laughing at him, Chris couldn't help noticing. He supposed he had that coming to him. He wasn't about to fault her. Besides, the veterinarian intrigued him as well as amused him.

He realized he couldn't wait for the wedding day to arrive because that meant he would have yet another opportunity to get together with everyone. Drilled with a sense of responsibility and a never-ending work ethic that wouldn't let up, Chris had to admit he couldn't remember ever feeling this way before.

The rancher turned his attention to his dinner and ate what was before him with gusto. Maybe it was his imagination, but everything he put into his mouth seemed to taste a lot better than the same fare ever had before.

Chapter Eight

"Well, there you go," Roe told the rancher as she brought Chris back to his vehicle in the church's parking lot. At this point, it was the only one that was still there. "Door-to-door service," she told him with a smile, adding, "It really doesn't get any better than that."

He had to agree with the woman he had chosen to be his veterinarian, but for entirely different reasons. He nodded his head.

"No, it doesn't." Getting out of the passenger side of her truck, Chris walked around toward the driver's side and stopped directly in front of her. "Thanks for this," he told her in all sincerity. "The wedding rehearsal and eating at the diner got my mind off potential other problems."

She knew he was referring to the possible infection that might be plaguing some of his cattle. Getting out of her truck for the moment, she felt for him. "There's been no word yet, so you still might wind up being in the clear. And if there is an infection," she said with confidence, "there are ways to handle it."

"No word yet," Chris echoed. "How would you know that?" he asked. "You were at the wedding rehearsal and then at the diner for the duration of the day."

"That doesn't mean I was unreachable. Unlike some people," Roe said, looking pointedly at the rancher, "I check my phone periodically for messages." She patted her purse where she kept her cell phone.

"And?" he pressed, wanting to hear the words that would put his mind at ease.

She could only tell him what she knew at the present moment. "And there weren't any."

Chris needed more. "Does that mean my cattle are in the clear?" he asked hopefully.

"No, that means Gene hasn't gotten back to me." The lab owner was exceedingly conscientious. It was the first thing she had learned about the older man when she became a vet.

"Jean?" Chris repeated. He was still relatively new to taking on all this responsibility at the ranch. "Is that her name?"

Roe smiled. It was a common mistake to make and it just meant that Chris hadn't had any dealings with the owner of the lab up to this point. His father had handled all those details until he had passed away.

"No, that's *his* name," she told the rancher. "Gene is a guy. He owns the lab. Took it over from his father." Her smile widened. "I guess that gives you two something in common."

Chris looked at her in surprise. "With everything that you have to do and take care of, how do you keep all these details straight in your head?"

She didn't see this as a reason to get confused. "It's really very simple. If I'm interested in something, then it's easy for me to remember," she told him cheerfully.

Chris nodded his head. "I'm beginning to think you're right." He realized that came out of left field so he explained, "I should get out more. It might help to expand my mind." His eyes met hers. "Thanks," he told her. "I had a really great time today."

It was nothing less than she had come to expect. "I'm very glad to hear that. But I kind of figured that you would," she told him. "I'm happy to be able to say that my family is made up of some of the nicest people you would ever want to meet."

He was not about to argue with that assessment. The rancher nodded. "I'm beginning to realize that." Pausing, he decided he had nothing to lose by asking, "You'll call me as soon as you hear anything about my cattle from this Gene person?"

"Count on it," Roe promised.

It occurred to her that she should get back into her truck. It also occurred to her that she was standing a lot closer to the rancher than she had been a few moments ago. So close that she could feel his breath on her upturned face when he spoke.

Not only that, but she could swear she felt something within her responding to him. That same sort of "something" she used to feel whenever their paths crossed in the school hallway all those years ago. Except that back then, she really didn't know what to expect or what to feel.

She did now.

Roe really couldn't say who made that first move, but before she knew it, the space between them was gone. Their lips had met and they were sharing the magnificent kiss that she had been fantasizing about since practically forever.

Her lips sealed to his and Roe rose up on her toes as far as she could. Her heart was hammering and slamming against her ribs.

Roe leaned into the sweet, almost overwhelming kiss that seemed to all but engulf her as it continued to mushroom and grow in proportion.

She could feel his mouth curving against hers.

Was he smiling?

Stepping back, she looked up with wonder at Chris, trying her best to understand what was happening. Why was he smiling?

"Did I do something to amuse you?" she asked.

He knew he had to tread very lightly here. The last thing he wanted was for her to think he was laughing at her.

"No. This has just turned out to be an unexpected

really nice evening," he confessed. "I didn't think it would be, but it's definitely a nice surprise. Thanks for the invitation and thanks for the ride back," he said, nodding toward his truck.

"Don't give it another thought," she told him. "And don't forget, you *are* invited to the actual wedding. And in the meantime, I'll give you a call regarding your cattle as soon as I have any information about them," she promised.

He nodded. "I'll be waiting for it."

She really hoped that the call would be one with good news to convey. She got back into her truck and started her vehicle, waving good-bye to Chris as she pulled out of the parking lot.

That had really turned out rather nicely, she thought, unconsciously running her fingers along her lips. Even better than she had thought it would.

Reaching her small house a few minutes later, she parked her truck in the driveway and walked to her front door.

The moment she opened it, she was greeted, as usual, with wagging tails and barely subdued, intense energy.

Roe laughed as she was surrounded by her pets, circling around her and voicing what she assumed was their version of a joyous greeting.

Every time she returned, the dogs acted as if she had been gone for weeks rather than just for a few hours. This time was no different.

"Yes, I missed you guys, too," she told the dogs,

doing her best to attempt to subdue them, at least a little bit. "And no, you're not going to get another meal out of me no matter how much you lick my face and nuzzle me. I left you a meal before I went to the rehearsal. It's not my fault you guys act like hungry vacuum cleaners set on high and suck up everything in sight within seconds.

"Now I'm going to fill your bowls with water—not food, water," she emphasized, "and then I don't know what you are going to do, but I am going to bed."

Kingston cocked his small white head as if he was really trying very hard to understand what she was telling him.

Roe merely smiled at the two dogs and poured more cold water into their water dishes—the bowls were almost empty—then made her way to her bedroom.

As she passed by the kitchen, she glanced toward the landline that was located there. She was disappointed to note that it wasn't blinking. She had given Gene the vials before going to the wedding rehearsal and he had promised to call her when he had results. He had both her landline number and cell phone number.

He hadn't called either one.

No news is good news, right? Roe asked herself. At least, that was true for tonight. She intended to focus on that.

Besides, she thought as she took off her maid of

honor dress and hung it up, then changed for bed, she had something else to focus on.

She snuggled into bed, thinking about Chris.

He had kissed her and she had definitely not been even the least bit disappointed. His kiss was every bit as wondrous and stimulating as she had imagined it might be.

Roe would have been the first one to admit she hadn't had all that much experience when it came to romance, and that included being kissed. For the most part, the kisses she had experienced were all right, but not exactly awe-inspiring. Her pulse hadn't gone into overdrive.

Until tonight.

Roe caught herself smiling again, *really* smiling. It felt as if her smile went all the way down to her toes, curling them.

The rancher really knew how to kiss, she mused, curling up against her pillow and holding it to her with a very contented sigh. She supposed that for some, kissing like that where it could awaken something wondrous within her, was just a spectacular inborn talent.

She couldn't wait until Riley and Matt's wedding arrived. Her pulse accelerated just by thinking about it. If nothing else, she promised herself to get Chris out on the dance floor. Roe didn't care how proficient the rancher was or wasn't when it came to dancing.

She just wanted to get him out there, holding her as they both swayed in time to the music.

The very thought of it made her smile.

Broadly.

The only thing that might ruin it, Roe thought, was if the lab results came in before then and it turned out to be bad news and not the good news they were both hoping for.

However, she told herself, she was not going to think about it until the bad news turned out to be a reality. The next best thing to good news was if the news did turn out to be bad, but only affected one of the animals and could, consequently, be easily cleared up.

Crossing her fingers, Roe curled up into her pillow again and, after a few minutes, fell fast asleep.

Lucy and Kingston woke her up the following morning in their usual fashion. They licked her cheeks and bounced around on her bed, one on either side of her.

Yawning, Roe stretched and tried to get her bearings. "I suppose I should be happy that you're both not wolfhounds," she said. Sitting up, she dragged her hand through her hair, still struggling to wake up. "Either of you take a phone message?" she asked with affection, ruffling the fur on both dogs' heads. "No? I didn't think so. Okay, boys and girls, off," she ordered, swinging her legs off the bed and getting up.

The German shepherd and Bichon Frisé scrambled off the bed and out of her way, at least for the moment. “I’ve got another busy day ahead of me, guys. Keep your little paws crossed for me that the news turns out to be good when I call the lab,” she told the dogs.

Roe hurried through her morning ritual moving even faster than usual. She kept checking her watch, aware of the fact that the lab opened at eight. However, Gene slept in the back area, behind the lab, so he would be able to hear the phone ringing if she was persistent.

She showered, dressed and put out the dogs’ food in a little over forty minutes, which left only making her bed.

“Move, Kingston,” she ordered as she pulled the blankets up. “Unless you have your heart set on getting trampled, or at the very least, folded up into my bed.”

The tiny dog seemed to understand the warning and practically leaped out of her way.

“Good boy,” she said with a laugh.

Roe remembered the days when Kingston was a puppy and had the terrible habit of weaving in and out around her legs, always managing to get underfoot. There were times when he came very close to tripping her—a lot of times, actually, she recalled. But she was nothing if not patient, and she always managed to train not just her own dogs, but dogs that belonged to other people as well. The dogs only had to be left in her care for a number of days or, at most, a number of weeks. At the end of that time, they wound up being trained and well behaved.

"Okay," she announced, setting down the things she had prepared. "There's your food, there's your water and there's the door. Time for me to make my exit." She looked over toward the silent landline.

No news is good news, she told herself again.

"Wish me luck, guys, and try not to get into any trouble," she said.

Roe was almost out the door, about to lock it, when she heard the landline ringing its high-pitched, shrill ring. Anticipation swept over her and she instantly became tense.

Most people no longer called the landline. That was for emergencies, when inclement weather would interfere with the cell phone reception, or telephone lines were being knocked down for some reason.

Most of the time, though, her calls came to her cell phone.

Gene at the lab was one of the few people she knew—practically the only one, she amended—who would get in contact with her using a landline. It turned out that he actually preferred using it. Gene was old-fashioned that way.

Her stomach instantly clenched.

"Showtime, guys," she told her pets. Glancing at the return number on the landline's screen, she saw that she was right. It was Gene calling her. She knew this was too early for his assistant to be calling. The man didn't get in until nine.

Roe crossed her fingers.

"This is Dr. Robertson," she told the caller needlessly. "How may I help you?"

Chapter Nine

"G'morning, Doc," she heard Gene Campbell's deep, raspy voice greeting her. "I've got good news and I've got bad news. Which would you like to hear first?"

"What I would really like to hear is that the news you have to tell me is all good," Roe told him.

"Sorry about that, Doc, but no can do. I'm not about to lie to you," Gene told her, sounding genuinely sorry.

She knew that he meant it. "I appreciate the position you're in, Gene." Roe sighed. "Well, since I have to pick one over the other, tell me the bad news first," Roe told the man she had known since even before she began studying veterinarian medicine in school.

She could almost hear the smile in his voice as he

said to her, "Always end on a high note, that's your motto, right, Doc?"

"You read my mind, Gene. Okay, so tell me, what's the bad news?" Roe asked, bracing herself and hoping that the bad news wasn't as terribly bad as it could be. She had turned over six vials of blood to the lab owner and was now sincerely praying that the vials were not all positive.

"Well, you were right," Gene informed her. "It's anemia."

"Oh lord," Roe groaned, envisioning what a really bad case of that meant.

"But out of the six vials you brought in for me to test," Gene quickly continued, tempering his bad news with the good news he had to offer, "only one of the vials proved to be positive for the infection. And, as we've already discussed, there's a way to treat that when the case isn't fatal. You perform a blood transfusion using healthy blood. And," he went on, "you also have to make sure that the tick population on the ranch in question is reduced and kept in check so that you don't encourage a fresh resurgence of the infection in the cattle being treated."

"In other words, make sure the owner of the herd follows common sense procedures," she told the lab owner, summing up the situation.

She heard Gene's deep chuckle. "In any words, common sense procedures," he agreed. "Have you got any questions for me, Doc?" Gene asked.

"No, not right now," she answered. "But I know where to find you if and when I do."

"Okay, then, keep me posted," he told her. "And if there is anything further that I can do for you, you said it yourself, you know where to find me."

She knew the man meant that. They had a very easy and good working relationship. "I appreciate that, Gene." Roe glanced at her watch. She needed to get going. "I'll see you at the wedding."

"Count on it. I'm really looking forward to it," he told her. "It's nice to do something normal. A man can only talk to his lab equipment for so long," Gene said.

Roe laughed. "We're going to have to do something about that when we get the chance," she told him. "But right now, I have to tell Chris Parnell that only one of his cows is sick and we have to make sure that what she has doesn't spread to the rest of the herd." It occurred to her that she didn't have a name yet. "Which one is it?" she asked.

"Rachel," he told her. Then, before she could ask if he was sure, he told her, "I tested the vial twice."

Roe nodded, even though the man couldn't see her. "Thanks for getting back to me so quickly."

"Hey, I live to serve," he said with a chuckle. "And don't forget to get back to me about your progress." He made it sound as if he fully expected there to be progress made dealing with the infection. That heartened her.

"Count on it," Roe promised.

Ending her call, she lost no time in placing a call to Chris. She knew he had to be eager to know the result of the vials that had been tested.

From what Chris had indicated to her, he was an early riser. If that was the case, he was undoubtedly already out of the house and most likely somewhere out on the range. Her only hope was that he was carrying his cell phone with him. He hadn't been the other day, of course, but with any luck, that had been an oversight on his part and the rancher had it with him today. The last thing she wanted to do today was go riding around looking for him the way she had to do the other day.

Besides, Roe reasoned, Chris knew the samples were at the lab to be tested. He had made it clear to her that he wanted to learn the outcome of the tests as soon as possible.

She knew—as did he—that they needed to get rolling once the test results were in. That way they ran a minimum of risk having the infection spread. That, in turn, meant she needed to get in contact with him as soon as she was able.

Roe tapped the rancher's cell phone number on her own phone, then listened to Chris's phone ring a number of times on the other end.

She grew more antsy and impatient with each ring.

And then she was listening to Chris's recorded voice telling her to please leave a message.

"I'll get back to you as soon as I can," the rancher promised just before ending the call.

"Oh no, not again," she cried, less than pleased. Roe swallowed several choice words that rose to her lips in the next few seconds.

Terminating the call, Roe immediately called the rancher's cell for a second time. She counted to herself as she listened to Chris's phone as it rang a total of eight times. And then she found herself listening to his recorded message. Again.

This time, she didn't just hang up. She left the rancher an annoyed message saying that if he didn't answer his phone the next time she called, when she got to the ranch and finally found him, she was planning on skinning him alive. "Slowly," she emphasized.

"And don't think I won't do it," she promised. "Just because we shared one hell of a great kiss the other night doesn't mean I won't skin you for getting in the way of my doing my job—and right now, you not picking up my call is seriously getting in the way of my doing my job," Roe bit off.

While talking to Chris on the phone, Roe had walked out of her house and gotten into her truck. She was currently attempting to curb her temper and not shout into her cell phone, but it definitely was not easy to do.

She was about to shut her phone for the third time when she thought she heard a noise coming from the phone's background. Something told her to wait another few seconds, although at this point, she was frustrated enough to toss her cell phone as far away from her as she possibly could.

Struggling to remain as calm as she could, she tightened her hand around her phone.

A deep male voice was saying "Hello?" into her ear.

It was just a single word, but she recognized Chris's voice immediately.

Well, it was about time, the veterinarian caught herself thinking even as she felt warm ripples going through her body.

"Hello," Roe responded. "Nice to see that you finally came out of your coma."

Her comment left the rancher somewhat confused. His phone crackled as he responded to ask, "What?"

Roe's hand was hovering over the car key she had just inserted into the ignition. Even though she was in a hurry, she refrained from turning the key. She was also struggling to hold onto her temper, which seemed to easily ignite today.

"I've been calling you and trying to reach you for the last twenty-some-odd minutes or so," she told him. "Talk about undertaking an exercise in futility."

His phone had been silent this morning. Chris took an educated guess as to why. This wasn't the first time it had been unreliable. "I'm sorry. The reception out here is spotty at times. I guess this was one of those times. My phone didn't ring this morning. Scout's honor."

Roe frowned, suppressing her sigh. Chris's genuine apology had taken the wind right out of her sails.

She couldn't be angry with the rancher if he hadn't meant for the oversight to happen.

She thought it best to get to the reason for her call. "I talked to the lab owner this morning. Gene processed the samples that I dropped off with him yesterday."

"And?" the rancher prodded nervously, barely able to get the question out. He felt as if his heart was lodged in his throat and growing bigger.

She felt for Chris, so she got this part out quickly so the rancher wasn't left hanging. "And it is anemia, just as we suspected. But so far, only one of your cows is infected," she told him.

"That's good, right?" Chris asked, not sure how to take this news. He was new to this part of ranching. He didn't want to jump the gun and view this as good news if it actually wasn't.

"Well, not for the cow," she told him honestly. "But for the rest of the herd, yes, it is. As long as we treat that cow, it's Rachel," she specified, "and keep the infection from getting worse, or spreading," she told him. "There's a good chance that we might even get the infection to clear up.

"Listen," Roe continued, "I'm about to head out to your ranch. Tell me where I can find you once I get there. I want to start Rachel's treatment immediately," she explained. "The sooner we start, the sooner we can eradicate it."

"That's great," he said, expressing his relief. Chris quickly rattled off his location.

Roe wrote down what he said in the margin of the paper she had been making notes on to herself. Finished, she told him, "I'll be there as soon as I can."

Still nervous, Chris found, to his embarrassment, that he needed a little more reassurance to cope with this situation. "So, it really is just Rachel?"

Roe could hear the questions the rancher wasn't asking. Whole herds had been known to be wiped out by various viruses that could spread through the animals like wildfire. It was an unspoken rule that a rancher's guard could never be dropped or relaxed until the day his whole herd was sold.

"That's what it looks like," she told Chris with confidence. "Don't worry," she assured him again, adding, "Gene is very good at what he does. He's worked with my grandfather's herd for years and Pop swears by the man. If he says it's just that one cow, then it's just that one cow."

"Well, that's good enough for me," the rancher told Roe. And then he thought of something. "Do you need me to do anything before you get here?"

"Just stay positive," she told him.

He laughed at her advice. "That is easier said than done."

"Yes," Roe agreed. "But it *can* be done," she assured the rancher. "I'm hanging up now, Chris," she told him, adding, "I drive better with two hands."

He was surprised that she wasn't using headphones. "You don't use any cute, gimmicky things for your cell phone?" he asked. For some reason, he could easily picture her doing that.

"Maybe later," she quipped. "But not right now. 'Bye," she told him. And then she terminated her call.

"Well, boss?" his ranch hand asked the moment Chris ended his call and tucked his cell phone into his back pocket.

Chris slid his hand over his back pocket to make sure the phone was safely in there. It was. "She's either trying to keep me from panicking until she gets here, or we don't have as much of a problem to worry about as I was afraid we had."

Jordan laughed dryly under his breath. "Well, I know what I'm hoping for," he told his boss.

"Yeah, you and me both," Chris answered.

Jordan looked at the herd. "She say which of the cows it was?" he asked.

All six of the cows had been separated from the rest of the herd just in case they turned out to actually be infectious. Even before he had taken over caring for the animals, Chris had slowly become familiar with all of them and was able to actually tell most of them apart from one another.

"She said it was Rachel," he told Jordan.

Jordan sighed. "It figures."

Chris knew what the ranch hand meant by that. Rachel was the smallest as well as the youngest of the herd and the wranglers were all rather partial to her.

"We'd better separate her from the others," Chris told the two wranglers with him.

"Did the doc say there was any hope that Rachel could lick this thing?" Jordan asked.

The other wrangler spoke up. He looked rather disturbed by what he had to relate. "I once saw a whole herd wiped out when they began to display signs of anemia."

Chris gave the man a censoring look. "Don't jinx this, Adams. The doc seems to have every hope that not only can she control this outbreak and keep it contained, but that she can cure Rachel as well."

"Hope she doesn't have to eat her words," Jordan spoke up.

"That makes two of us," Adams said quietly to the other wrangler.

"Three of us," Chris added. He knew that in their own way, the wranglers were as invested in a positive outcome with the herd as he was.

Chapter Ten

"You made great time," Chis commented, riding up to Roe's truck the moment he saw her driving onto his property.

Seeing him, the veterinarian pulled her truck over to one side. Stopping it, she got out.

"To be honest, I didn't feel like we had any time to waste. The faster we treat this infection, the better off we will all be." Roe looked at the two wranglers Chris had working with him on the range this morning. They looked properly dedicated, which she found heartening. That was not always the case when it came to wranglers working on a ranch. "Your men are going to need to isolate Rachel from the rest of the herd so her infection doesn't get a chance to spread to the others," she told him. "According to the tests, none of the other cattle have come down with the infection. She seems to be the only one. Are you able to gauge just how long Rachel has had this anemia?" she asked Chris. "When did you first notice that she was showing signs of having something wrong?"

He thought for a moment, trying to tie the infection to an event. He couldn't actually pin it down accurately. "About a week. No more than eight or nine days tops," he told Roe. "And even then, I really wasn't sure that she had anything," Chris confessed. The rancher searched the veterinarian's face, looking for his own answers. "Is she going to be all right?" he asked. "And just as importantly, is the rest of the herd going to be all right?"

"We're going to try to do our utmost best to make sure this infection isn't going to spread," Roe promised the rancher.

She proceeded to take out a bottle of fluid from her medical bag, along with the tubes she was going to need to insert into the cow so that the bad blood could be drawn and then eventually exchanged for the good blood.

"This looks like something straight out of a hospital," Chris commented, looking at the tubes she had laid out on a clean sheet before her.

"It very well could be," Roe assured him. Heaven knew she tried to keep everything she used neat and clean. And then she looked up at Chris and his wranglers. In order to work, this procedure was going to have to involve all of them. "Okay, boys, Rachel is not going to be a happy camper about being used as a pincushion, but in order for her to have a chance to get better, this really has to be done. The three of you have to hold onto her while I'm the one who gets to draw out the bad blood, and then put in the good blood."

Jordan laughed under his breath. "You're right. She is definitely not going to be happy about this," the wrangler commented, looking at the thick tubing.

Roe had taken out a vial of serum and was drawing it in order to inject into the cow. "That's why I'm going to tranquilize her first so that she's a little easier to work with. Otherwise, she's going to buck and kick all four of us, possibly to the point of making us all senseless," Roe warned the men.

The news amazed the rancher. "She'd kick you, too?" Chris asked her.

"Hey, she's not about to single me out for any special treatment," Roe told the rancher. "If anything, she might wind up blaming me more."

Chris seemed rather amazed by all this. "You make it sound like Rachel is actually capable of having a thought process."

Roe was still preparing the tubing to make sure that the blood was able to flow through it and into the cow's upper thigh. She gave him a look. "That's because she is," she told Chris.

Jordan's brows drew together in a wavy, hairy line

as he fixed her with a look. "You're kidding, right?" the wrangler asked her.

"No, I'm not," she informed the wrangler seriously. "All animals are capable of thinking to a greater or less degree."

Examining the tubing one last time, Roe was satisfied that the blood would be able to flow easily from the vial into the cow's limb.

"Okay, I'm ready," she declared. "Hold her like *my* life depended on it," she emphasized.

"But you tranquilized her," Chris protested, pointing to the vial she had used.

"Doesn't mean she still can't give me one hell of a swift kick and a really big bruise," Roe told the rancher and the other men. "And since I'm going to be in my sister's wedding party in a couple of days, I would really rather not look as if I came off like the loser in a boxing match." Her eyes swept over each of the men to see if they got her point.

"Okay, men," Chris announced to his wranglers, "you heard the lady. Hold onto Rachel as if your very lives depended on it."

She flashed the rancher a very grateful smile. Then, taking in a deep breath, Roe braced herself and asked, "Ready?"

"Ready," all three men declared almost at the same time.

Rachel made what passed for a frightened noise as all three men held onto a different part of the cow. Rachel was rather small for a cow, but she was still large enough to be a challenge for the ranch hands to hold onto, especially since Roe hadn't elected to put her out completely.

Several minutes of wrestling and holding down different parts of the cow led to eventually being able to hold Rachel still—or as still as they possibly could.

The transfusion took a while to complete. Finally finished, Roe was able to sigh deeply, exhausted from the whole ordeal of wrestling and attempting to subdue the remarkably strong animal.

Roe was also fairly wet. Holding Rachel turned out to be very sweaty work. Looking at the cow now, Roe couldn't help but smile. "I think the transfusion was successful," she told Chris. "She seems to be on the road to recovery."

He was leaning up against the cow and appeared to be just as exhausted as she and his men were. The rancher almost laughed out loud.

"How can you tell?" he asked, tongue-in-cheek.

"Practice," she told him, as she looked at Rachel. "Lots and lots of practice."

"I'll take your word for it," Chris told the veterinarian. Straightening up, he glanced at Roe. "Are you finished?"

"Well, for the most part. The only thing left to do is observe Rachel for a little while to make sure there are no bad side effects to the medication and that the medication and transfusion worked."

Roe began to get to her feet. The rancher had gotten to his first, so he offered her a hand. Roe smiled at him and then wrapped her fingers around the extended hand as he all but pulled her up to her feet.

His eyes skimmed over her. For the most part, she looked disheveled, but she still looked quite beautiful. "Would you like to wash up?" Chris suggested.

A grin played along her lips. "Is that your polite way of telling me that I look sweaty and messy?"

He appeared stunned at her takeaway. He hadn't meant to insult her, but he knew if he protested too much, his words would only turn around to bite him.

"That's my awkward way of offering you some water so you could clean up a little," the rancher answered.

Roe laughed. "I'll definitely take it," she told him. She brushed off her hands. "Okay, lead the way to your ranch house."

Chris nodded agreeably, happy he hadn't accidentally insulted her, because that certainly hadn't been his intention.

"Just follow me," he told her, pointing out the house and beginning to ride in that direction.

She wanted to tell him that it would be quicker driving there than using a horse, but she refrained. He was the rancher, so she took the hand he offered her and got on his horse behind him.

Upon arrival, she saw that Chris's family ranch house was smaller than the one her grandfather had built, but then her mother had told her that Pop had added on to the house when she and her sisters had come along. From what Roe had gathered, when it came to Chris's property, his father had never had a reason to add onto it, or even to remodel any part of it.

As a matter of fact, after his father had died, there had been serious talk about selling the ranch, especially when his mother decided to move on with her life. And as for Chris's older brother, Pete, he wanted nothing to do with the ranch. Unlike Chris, he wasn't interest in taking care of cattle or anything else that was ranch related. The sooner Pete could get out of there with money in his pocket, the better.

Chris, however, had an affinity for the property.

"Cozy," Roe commented as she got off Chris's horse and looked over the front of the ranch.

Chris shrugged at what he took to be a compliment. "It needs work."

She laughed at his disparaging tone. "Everything needs work," she told him. "But along with work, you just need to devote a certain amount of love to it." She began making a checklist in her head, then stopped herself. She didn't want to wind up overwhelming him.

Gesturing toward the house, she said, "Okay, lead the way."

Chris opened the door, then held it for her. Since she was there to clean herself up, he asked Roe, "Do you want to use the kitchen or the bathroom?"

She wasn't focusing on sprucing herself up too much. "I just want to wash my hands, so I'll take the kitchen," she told Chris.

Obliging, Chris led her to the kitchen.

He picked up a kitchen towel and handed it to her. "Soap's right there. Anything else?"

"Nope, I'm good," she responded, beginning to run the water. She took the bar of soap and proceeded to lather her hands.

"Yes, you certainly are," the rancher said. There was a broad smile not just on his lips but shining in his eyes as well.

Although she liked being complimented, she didn't respond to receiving empty compliments for no reason. "Save that for when we're sure the danger of a blood infection has passed."

He supposed that made sense. Chris nodded, then remembered what she had said about waiting to see if the medication would take effect. "Are you planning on hanging around?"

"For a while, yes," she told him. "At least until I feel that we've partially gotten out of the woods with Rachel. If you have somewhere else to be, don't let me stop you," she told him. "This won't be the first time I kept watch over a sick animal."

He shook his head, dismissing her suggestion. "I'm all yours," he told her. Then, realizing how that had to have sounded, he amended his words. "Whatever you need, I'm at your disposal. After all," he reminded her, "these are my cattle. I'm not planning on just throwing up my hands and walking away."

"I didn't mean to suggest that you were," she said. "Just that you might be busy attending to some other ranch matters."

He laughed. "And you're not?" It was a rhetorical question on his part.

She realized that being around him caused her to be tongue-tied at times. "I didn't mean it that way."

"I know that. It wasn't meant to be an insult," Chris told her.

She shook her head. "You know, I don't remember things being so awkward between us when we were in school."

"Well, you're doing a lot better than I am because I don't remember there even being an 'us,'" he told the veterinarian. He actually did, but he didn't want to scare her off.

She merely smiled. "That's because guys don't remember things like that."

"Was that a put-down?" he asked her, his brow wrinkling, curious as to her intent.

"Nope, just a simple statement of fact," Roe told the rancher. Finished washing up, she dried her hands. "Well, I don't know about you, but I have a cow waiting for me to put in an appearance so I need to be getting back to the barn to make sure everything's still going as well as we'd hoped."

He inclined his head. "Then let's get going," Chris agreed. "I'll lead the way," he offered, hurrying back to where he had left his horse tethered.

They got back to the barn quickly enough. Rachel seemed to be coming out of her drug-induced lethargy. Roe lost no time in getting over to the cow she had sedated earlier in the day.

"Isn't the effect of the sedation supposed to last longer than this?" Chris asked, joining her at the stall.

Roe smiled down at the cow. "Usually. But I didn't give her that much medication, just enough to keep her from butting her head at me while I was doing her transfusion," she told the rancher. "I didn't want her to be overly groggy."

The rancher nodded. "I guess that makes sense," Chris commented.

She glanced at him. There was laughter in her eyes for his grudgingly voiced approval. "Thank you," she said.

Chris looked over his shoulder, back at Rachel. "So what now?" he asked.

"We watch her. Give her water to drink. Make sure she doesn't throw up and all sorts of good things like that," she told the rancher, humor curving her mouth. "You can get comfortable," she suggested. "Or..." Her voice trailed off as she gave him a look.

She was leaving the final decision up to him, Chris realized.

He liked working with her. She didn't act superior because of all the information that was in her head. He liked that as well.

"I'll take getting comfortable," he told the veterinarian, picking his choice.

She nodded her head at what he had just said. She gestured toward the back of the stall and made herself comfortable outside of the area that the cow was currently in.

There was nothing left to do but wait. With luck, the cow would continue to be all right.

Mentally, she crossed her fingers and settled in to enjoy the company that was there.

Chapter Eleven

Roe glanced at her watch. She had been out here on the ranch for several hours now and the tranquilized young cow had, at this point, officially become exceptionally restless. As much as she liked being here, talking to the rancher about a whole variety of different subjects, it was time for her to get going, Roe decided. She had other things to do.

"I think we're out of the woods," she announced to the rancher. She got back up to her feet and brushed the straw off her jeans.

Chris was right behind her, rising to his feet as well. "You're sure?" he asked her as he looked rather uncertainly at the cow.

"Well, as sure as I can be," she told the rancher. "I want you and your men to keep an eye on Rachel for the next few days. Treat the area where she grazes for ticks. And, if you see any signs that make you feel that she might be relapsing, you know where to find me." Roe smiled encouragingly at him, fairly confident that everything was going to be all right.

Chris walked the veterinarian to her truck, giving one of his wranglers who looked at him quizzically a thumbs-up sign. It was to indicate that everything looked as if it was going to be all right.

"I can't thank you enough for everything you've done," he said.

Roe stopped beside her vehicle as she shrugged off his thanks. "Well, I'd be a really poor excuse for a veterinarian if I hadn't tried to bring Rachel around." She flashed another smile at the rancher. "It's what I was born to do," she told him in all seriousness. "As a matter of fact, I never even considered doing anything else than what I'm doing right now."

"Lucky for me—and my cattle," Chris said. And then he realized something. "We still haven't discussed my paying you. I fully intend to," he assured her again, then told her, "It just won't be all at once." And then he tried to pin her down for the information he was missing. "You still haven't told me how much that is going to be."

She was completely aware of that. Roe hadn't been able to find the time to draw up a proper bill and she definitely was not in any hurry to do so.

"I'll send you a bill when I get a chance to write it up and then we'll discuss payment," she told him.

"Right now, I need to get home to Kingston and Lucy. They don't like it when I'm gone all day."

"Kingston and Lucy?" the rancher questioned, then made a guess. "Your horses?"

"My dogs," the veterinarian corrected. "They keep one another company, but they're not exactly overly thrilled whenever I leave the house. My guess is that it seems like hours to them."

"What kind of dogs are they?" Chris asked, curious.

"Noisy ones," she answered with a laugh. "Maybe you could come over and meet them someday."

Until recently, the rancher had had a pet dog himself. But Brutus had died a little more than three months ago. Chris still found himself missing the pet a great deal. Roe's suggestion about meeting her dogs made him smile.

"I'd like that," he told Roe. "Maybe I can come by and pick you up the day of the wedding. I can meet your dogs then."

Under normal circumstances, that would have been a really good idea, she thought. But as it stood now, there were obstacles for her to deal with on the appointed wedding day.

"That's not going to work out because I'm going to have to be at the church along with the rest of the wedding party early that day. Maybe we can do that after the wedding is all over," she suggested.

A smile curved his mouth. "Okay, I'll pencil that

in on my calendar," he told her, pretending to be serious.

Roe inclined her head as she got back into her vehicle. "I'll let the dogs know. They'll be looking forward to seeing you," she told Chris, amused at the thought of what he might be thinking.

Chris nodded, happy to take her up on it. "Sounds good to me."

The rancher watched Roe pull away in her truck and get on the road.

That had turned out pretty well on all counts, he thought. Luckily, the infection hadn't spread to any of the rest of the herd and from all indications, it appeared Rachel had contracted what seemed like a very mild case of anemia.

Roe was very aware of the bullet that had just been dodged by Chris's herd.

For now she needed to gather her thoughts together and focus on what else was going on around her.

Like Riley's wedding.

She couldn't wait for the wedding to take place. The added bonus in her case was that she had managed to convince Chris to attend the wedding. Not just the ceremony but the actual celebration after the wedding vows were exchanged. That was a pretty good accomplishment.

Even so, Roe could feel her stomach muscles tighten. She could feel herself anticipating the entire event, including after the ceremony. Still a couple of days away, she was definitely getting excited about it.

Moving quickly, Roe swung by her house to check on her dogs. Because she was due at her grandfather's house along with the rest of the wedding party, she could only spare a few minutes, but she was not about to miss looking in on her dogs.

"Did you guys miss me?" Roe asked them as she opened the front door. "I missed you."

She barely got the words out before she was swarmed by the two dogs eagerly coming at her from both sides, bounding around and licking her to show how happy they were to see her.

Roe sank down on the floor between them, petting them and laughing with pleasure. After the day she had, it was almost therapeutic.

It really felt good to forget about everything else and just enjoy the way the dogs eagerly sought her attention, pushing each other out of the way and showing the extent of their love for her.

This was her real reward for all the hard work she put in, Roe thought, garnering the love of her pet dogs.

Deciding that she needed to get going, she finally got up off the floor. Roe checked the dogs' water bowls. "You practically drank everything," she commented. "Let me fill your bowls and then I have to go. Pop wants us all there for dinner," she told the dogs. "Sorry, but you guys aren't included." A sympathetic expression came over her face. She could almost feel their sadness at being left out. "Maybe next time."

Lucy barked at her, as if in response. Roe just laughed at the shepherd and stroked the dog's head.

Kingston wiggled in between Lucy and his mistress, claiming a space.

Roe ran her hand over the shorter dog's head as well, then she headed for the front door. "Gotta go, guys. Be good. I'll see you later," she told the pets as she left the house again.

Getting back into her truck, the veterinarian drove to the ranch house where she had grown up. It had already been a very busy day, and she could have easily just made herself a little dinner, and then gone off to bed sooner rather than later. But she had to admit she did like the idea of getting together with her family, despite the fact that they had dinner together every Sunday.

The way Pop had worded his invitation, he'd said he wanted to see their "bright, shining faces, sitting at his table and breaking bread with him and their mother."

That was not the sort of invitation Roe and her sisters would readily ignored, nor would they have wanted to.

Neither would the two men who had chosen to be Raegan's and Riley's "other halves." Not to mention that Vikki was being included as well, Roe thought with a smile, and she absolutely *loved* having the little girl around.

Stepping on the gas, Roe drove a little faster than she normally would, exceeding the speed limit by a little. But then, there wasn't exactly any traffic to get in her way, as long as she was careful and kept her eyes opened.

When she arrived, Roe noticed from the cars parked there that her sisters, as well as Alan and Matt, had all gotten there ahead of her.

Par for the course, she mused.

But there was one other truck parked in the driveway as well.

Roe's heart began to pound harder as recognition set in. Except that she had to be wrong, Roe told herself. That car couldn't belong to who she thought it belonged to.

Could it?

Parking her truck as close to the other truck as she could, Roe got out. She gave the other truck a slow once-over to determine whether or not she was wrong.

Her mouth went dry as she realized that she wasn't wrong.

The first thing that occurred to Roe was there had either been a resurgence of the infection that appeared to have plagued Rachel, or another problem had suddenly arisen and Chris hadn't been able to reach her to tell her about it.

How had he known to come here?

Her breath lodged in her throat, Roe all but flew to the front door. Opening it, she hurried into the ranch house.

"What happened?" she cried as she quickly made her way into the living room.

Her grandfather was there, talking to the people who he had invited into his home for dinner. He momentarily stopped talking to turn around and look at Roe.

Her words caught him off guard. "Did I miss something? Is this the new way to say 'hello?'" Mike Robertson asked.

Roe tried to be more clear regarding the question. "Did Rachel have a relapse?" she asked Chris.

"No," the rancher quickly assured her. And then he said, "You didn't know? Your grandfather invited me to dinner."

Roe turned to look at her grandfather. "Pop?" she asked quizzically.

"Yes, I invited him to have dinner with the family," Mike confirmed. "I didn't realize I needed to ask you for permission."

Roe took a deep breath, doing her best to calm her nerves down.

"I didn't mean to insinuate that you had to do that," she quickly told the older man. "It's just that you never asked him to come over before and since I spent the day watching over a cow in his herd to make sure she didn't show any further signs of having an infection, I thought there had to be something wrong with his cattle for him to show up this way."

"I'm sorry. I didn't mean to make you think the worst. I was trying to do something nice for everyone and just have an even number of guests at the table," her grandfather explained.

Roe felt embarrassed about her mistake. "Sorry," she apologized, looking at her grandfather and then at Chris. "I guess I was just prepared for the worst when I saw your truck." She sank down at the table. "So Rachel's all right?" she asked Chris, just to be sure.

"Rachel has never been better," the rancher assured her with feeling. "I left her looking like she was an eager calf," he confessed.

Roe looked at her grandfather, then began to explain the situation to him. "Chris called me in to examine some of his herd. I thought they might be coming down with anemia. It turned out that only one cow had it and I treated her with a blood transfusion. I think we managed to get the infection before it spread through his herd and infected any of the other cattle," she proudly told her grandfather.

Mike nodded his head. "You are the best, Roe," he said proudly, his eyes meeting hers. "But you should be aware that even the best have setbacks once in a while."

She nodded, accepting the praise and the fact that it was being tempered. "Just luckily not this time," she told her grandfather.

Mike looked at the rest of his family. "Sit, people. The food's not coming out until you're all seated," he told them. When they complied, he nodded his head and called out, "All right, Rosa, time to serve your wonderful meal."

Taking her seat beside the rancher she had just recently left on his ranch, she lowered her voice and asked him, “Why didn’t you tell me you were coming to my grandfather’s ranch for dinner tonight?”

“Because I didn’t know I was when you were at my place,” he explained. “Your grandfather contacted me after you had already left to go back to town,” Chris informed her. “To be honest, you could have knocked me over with a feather when he called,” he said. “If anything, I would have expected the invitation to come from you, not your grandfather.”

“Pop?” she asked looking at her grandfather.

He shrugged as he began to cut the meat Rosa had just brought in and placed directly in front of him.

“I like even numbers at the table,” he told Roe, not for the first time. “Sue me.”

Carving more portions, he distributed the meat equally amid the people seated at his table. “Eat up, people,” Mike urged. “After all, you don’t want to insult Rosa,” he told his guest and his family members, the latter of which were well aware of how to behave around the woman who had cooked all their meals for them for more years than they could remember.

Chapter Twelve

When he sat down at the table, Chris had assumed that dinner at the Robertsons' home would be very pleasant and most likely very tasty, as well as a rather quick, rather quiet affair meant to feed the body as well as the soul.

Instead, the humor-laced conversation around the table actually lasted for several hours.

The rancher caught himself smiling broadly a number of times at what was being said. In addition, Chris really couldn't remember the last time he had enjoyed himself to this extent.

It wasn't just Roe who made him feel this bright and sunny inside, although she was responsible for a very large part of his feeling like this. In reality it was actually the entire family who contributed to this feeling of overall general wellbeing and contentment.

The triplets' mother, Rita, smiled as she looked across the table, taking both Chris and his clean dinner plate into account. Pleased, Rita Robertson had to admit that she had hardly seen the young rancher's fork moving, but it had to have been exceptionally fast.

"Would you like to have another serving of roast beef, Christopher?" she asked the rancher. When Chris protested that he didn't want to be responsible for cleaning them all out of food, Roe's mother said, "I'm sure that Rosa has set aside the usual leftovers for Pop to use for his midnight snack, so there is still plenty of food to go around."

Mike sighed as he shook his head. "There you go again, Rita, giving away all my secrets," Mike said, pretending to complain to his daughter-in-law.

"I'm sure that Christopher was not about to accuse you of harboring some sort of secret plan," Rita told her father-in-law with an amused laugh.

Chris was all but beaming with pleasure as he spoke to his host and hostess. "Please tell Rosa that I thought dinner was absolutely magnificent."

Mike laughed. "Oh, I think after all these years of making the girls salivate while she was cooking, Rosa knows all she has to do is to bring out a meal that she's prepared and she would have the girls' mouths watering."

Rita gave her father-in-law a long, penetrating

look. "Just the girls?" she asked pointedly, her meaning very clear.

Mike shrugged as he innocently glanced around the table. "Well, I guess you could include their other halves as well," the girls' grandfather allowed magnanimously.

Roe tilted her head as she looked back at her grandfather. "Can you say that again, Pop?" she requested innocently. "I missed seeing your nose growing that time," the veterinarian said, "And I really hate missing that."

Mike pretended to scowl at Roe as his features deliberately assumed a frown. "Very funny, little girl."

"She's not a little girl, Grandpop," Vikki told him as she raised her voice and spoke up, proudly informing the man of this small piece of information. Jerking her thumb at her chest, she said, "I am."

Vikki never failed to tickle the triplets' grandfather whenever she pointed something out for the older man's attention.

"Yes, you're right. My mistake," Mike admitted. "You certainly are that little girl," he agreed. "As a matter of fact, you are my very favorite little girl in the whole world."

Vikki began to giggle in response, which in turn had the girls' grandfather bestowing a very warm, heartfelt embrace on her as well as softly kissing her cheek. Her cheeks turned an endearing shade of pink in response.

Looking toward Chris to see how he was taking all

this in, Roe was pleased to see him smiling broadly at the displays of affection.

Chris leaned in and asked Roe, "Whose little girl is she?" The rancher realized he hadn't been told whose daughter she actually was and he found himself curious as to where the little girl fit into this family structure.

Roe kept her face turned away from the others so that her voice wouldn't carry too far. "She is the daughter of Riley's late best friend, Breena. Breena died from cancer a little more than six months ago," she explained. "Breena really wanted Vikki to get to know her father."

"And that is?" Chris asked.

Roe smiled. "Vikki was the product of a beautiful summer romance between Breena and Matt." She nodded her head toward the engineer. "Except that he didn't know it at the time."

Chris looked at her quizzically. This was all new to him. Picking up on his look, Roe continued explaining. "At the time, Breena knew that Matt had plans to go into engineering once he got his degree and she didn't want to interfere with those plans. She certainly didn't want him to feel that he was obligated to marry her because they had unwittingly created a child together. So when he wrote to her, she didn't answer any of his letters and just went on with her life. I doubt she would have ever told him about Vikki if she hadn't found out she was dying."

Roe took a deep breath and continued. "She had

Riley write a letter to Matt for her posthumously, letting him know that she had given birth to his child and he needed to come out to Forever to at least get to know Vikki." She smiled, recalling the incident. "Matt came as soon as he received the letter. He was absolutely stunned. But he did come immediately."

"But Vikki's mother had already died?" the rancher asked, trying to keep the details straight.

Roe nodded. "She had," the veterinarian confirmed sadly.

This wasn't making any sense to the rancher. "But I saw the wedding party at the rehearsal. How did Matt's bride-to-be wind up being Riley?" he asked. That part just wasn't making any sense to him.

"Well, it is rather a strange story," Roe admitted. "I told you that my sister, Riley, was Breena's best friend. She stood by Breena throughout the entire pregnancy, Vikki's birth and afterward. And while Breena never listened to a single bad word spoken against Matt, she did talk about him in warm, kind terms to Riley.

"Listening to words to that effect, somewhere along the way I think Riley just wound up falling for Vikki's father." Roe smiled at the memory of that evolution. "Right now it's almost as if the soul of Breena existed there in spirit as a go-between for Riley and Matt. So it was really no surprise to anyone when they announced they were getting married," she told Chris.

"It didn't surprise anyone?" Chris questioned in amazement.

"Nope. The only thing that really mattered was that Vikki was comfortable with what was taking place, both with Matt, her father, and Riley, who she had known her entire life. She is a lovable little girl and she loves my entire family. And they, in turn, love her.

"And somewhere," Roe said confidently as she waved her hand above her head, "Breena is looking down on all this and she is smiling broadly."

Finished with the tale of her family, Roe paused for a moment, looking at the rancher and waiting for him to absorb the story. When he made no comment, she asked him, "Would you like to have some dessert?"

Chris rested his hand on his stomach as he rolled his eyes. "I'm not all that sure I can fit any dessert in," he commented to her. "That second helping of roast beef wound up taking up all the available space I had," the rancher told her.

Rita overheard what Chris had said to Roe about dessert. "Oh, Rosa is serving ice cream, young man. There is *always* room for ice cream," the girls' mother assured him.

Chris didn't want to say "no" to the woman, but he didn't want to leave anything behind on his plate or in his bowl. He had been raised to always clear his plate. "All right, I'll just have a small bowl then," he told Roe's mother, then underscored, "A *very* small bowl."

Rita glanced at her father-in-law, smiling. "More for you, right, Pop?" she asked.

"Right," Pop agreed with a large grin. "And don't make mine a small bowl," he cautioned. "I can *always* eat.

The bowls of mint chip ice cream were quickly doled out. Most of the bowls contained more than a double portion of the ice cream—except for Chris's.

Rita looked at the rancher dubiously as she dished out the frozen treat. "Are you sure this will be enough for you?"

"Absolutely, ma'am," Chris assured her. "I wasn't kidding about being stuffed, Mrs. Robertson." His eyes met hers as he crossed his heart to underscore his point.

"I wouldn't want you leaving here with any complaints about the amount of food and certainly not the service," Rita informed him, following her words with a broad wink.

"I would never complain, Mrs. Robertson," Chris assured the triplets' mother, "especially since everything that was served in abundance tasted so good."

Rita laughed. "I promise that I intend to hold you to that, young man."

"Yes, ma'am," Chris replied, looking at the older woman with a very serious expression on his face.

Another hour went by. Roe looked at her watch, then at Chris. "Are you ready to leave yet?" she asked the rancher quietly.

"Oh, by the way, here's your hat. What's your

hurry?" her grandfather teased with a laugh and then winked at Chris.

"I didn't mean it that way, Pop," Roe told her grandfather. "But you're a rancher. You know how important it is to be able to get up early so you can start working early, right?" she questioned her grandfather.

"Roe is right, Pop," Riley told their grandfather. "We're going to have to be leaving, too. Especially with Vikki here almost falling asleep at the table," Riley said, nodding at the little girl.

"She does have a point, sir," Matt told his future grandfather-in-law, sliding his sleeping daughter onto his lap.

Vikki murmured something in her sleep, then sighed as she rested her head against her father's shoulder, totally sound asleep.

"Well, I certainly can't argue with that," Mike agreed as he looked around at the tired faces at the table. "You're all sleeping beauties," Mike told the two couples. "Go home." Mike Robertson looked at Raegan and her husband. "How about you two? Are you tired and going home as well?"

"I think we should be, Pop" Raegan agreed. "Alan is trying to make up for the time he's taking off for this wedding."

Mike laughed to himself as he shook his head. "Well, they certainly don't make young people like they used to. Was a time I could stay out all night," he told the six young people who were seated at his table. His assessment took in his daughter-in-law and

Vikki as well. "And then get up early in the morning to get to work. Right, Rita?" Mike asked pointedly, looking directly at his late son's widow.

"If you say so, Pop," his daughter-in-law responded good-naturedly.

"Not exactly a rip-roaring testimonial," Mike bemoaned, "But for now, I guess it'll have to do."

He rose to his feet, following the group out of the house and to their cars. "Drive home safely," he cautioned.

Riley smiled at her grandfather. "We'll do our best, Pop," she told him as they all made their way to their separate vehicles.

Chapter Thirteen

When they left the Robertson ranch house, two of the three couples, plus Vikki, were all planning on driving home.

Having arrived separately, Chris and Roe were both going toward their own trucks, intent on going home as well. The veterinarian abruptly stopped walking and turned toward Chris. The others stopped as well.

"Something wrong?" Christopher asked.

"No." Roe shook her head. "But I've got an idea. Would you like to follow me into town and meet my dogs? I have a feeling they would really like to meet you."

Chris paused next to his truck and gave her a rather curious look. "And you know that for a fact?" he asked, fighting to keep the smile from his face. "Did they come out and tell you that?"

Roe grinned widely at the rancher. "In a manner of speaking," she admitted. When he looked at her oddly, she told him, "When you spend time with certain animals, you get pretty good at what's on their minds and guessing what they're thinking."

Chris had his doubts about that, but he had to admit she had been fairly good at arriving at the right conclusions when it came to curing his cow. That was good enough for him, Chris decided.

"Is that a fact?" Chris asked the vet, amusement curving his mouth.

"Oh, absolutely," Roe assured him with a certainty that Chris had to admit he found rather difficult to argue with. Roe seemed nothing if not positive about her conclusion, especially when it involved animals.

About to say something to her, the rancher glanced at his watch. He didn't usually call it a night this early in the evening. It felt pretty good stretching his muscles this way, he thought.

All in all, he had to admit that he had a very good time this evening. With that in mind, he turned toward Mike Robertson and Mike's daughter-in-law, Rita.

"Thank you for having me over, Mr. Robertson. Mrs. Robertson," he said, inclining his head toward first Rita, then Mike. "I had a really great time. As a matter of fact, I can't remember the last time I enjoyed myself as much as I did this evening," the rancher admitted to the duo.

Rita smiled brightly at the rancher. "Well, that just means we're going to have to invite you over more often," she told Chris. "Right, Pop?" she asked, turning toward her father-in-law.

"Right," the older man agreed. "And let's not forget, we'll be seeing you at the wedding on Saturday. From what I know, Roe doesn't have a date yet, do you, Roe? So you can just stand in as her escort, right, Chris?"

The three sisters expressed their shock—as well as their dismay—over this revelation being made to someone they didn't know well about Roe's situation.

"What?" Mike asked, looking from one granddaughter to the next and appearing surprised by their reactions. He shrugged his shoulders. "I'm just confirming the fact that Roe is very picky when it comes to agreeing to going *anywhere* with an escort. To my way of thinking, this would solve that problem," the girls' grandfather confirmed with satisfaction, nodding his head. He pinned Roe with a look.

She felt she had pushed her luck far enough.

"And on that note," Roe announced as she turned toward her truck, "Chris and I will be saying goodnight." And then she turned toward Chris as he opened the driver's side door to his truck, waiting for him to say something.

"So, do you want me to follow you into town?"

he asked, then explained, "That way I can meet your posse?"

She liked the way a glimmer of amusement had entered the rancher's eyes as he spoke.

She thought that his following her into town was a good idea and explained why. "It's dark and you're not all that familiar with finding your way around town." So yes, that would be my suggestion."

Chris turned back toward the pair standing at the front of the house one last time. He said his good-byes to Roe's mother and grandfather.

"Again, thank you for having me over for dinner, and I will see you all at the church the day of the wedding," he told the family members, shaking each of their hands.

Not to be left out, Vikki presented herself in front of her father's new friend, her small hand extended out to him. "See you at the church."

"Absolutely," Chris promised sincerely, finding himself completely captivated by the very animated little girl.

"Okay," the rancher announced to the veterinarian as he got into his truck, "lead the way."

Nodding, she did just that. Roe had been drive for less than fifteen minutes when a bolt of lightning lit up the sky.

The lightning bolt was so bright that it almost looked as if the surrounding area was bordering on daylight.

Her car window was open and the very air smelled like pending rain.

Trying to outrace the raindrops, she stepped harder on the gas pedal, wanting to reach her house before the rain broke.

A few moments later, after she and Chris arrived on her front porch, another streak of lightning creased the brow of the sky and then suddenly it began pouring rain.

Roe put her key into the door, then glanced in Chris's direction. "Brace yourself," she warned.

He thought she was telling him to brace himself for the rain that had already started.

"It's already raining," he told her. He had his doubts that it could rain any harder.

"I'm not talking about that," she told him. Roe glanced at the rancher to make sure he was prepared, and then she turned the doorknob and pushed open the front door. Simultaneously she called out, "Okay, I brought him with me, Remember our deal. You're supposed to behave yourselves and not scare him away!"

For half a second, Chris thought she was talking to him—and then he realized that Roe was issuing the warning to the two whirling balls of fluff—one small, one large—that ran by her and were now circling madly around him.

"Stay calm!" she warned him, putting her hand on his arm in a comforting manner. "Stay calm!"

He was about to ask her why she felt compelled to issue that warning, but then he had his answer.

Chris found he could barely remain upright, surrounded the way he was by Kingston and Lucy, both of them barking madly.

Because she was worried that Lucy, the German shepherd, would wind up knocking Chris over, she grabbed the dog's collar and held onto her tightly and with all her might.

"Down, Lucy, down!" Roe ordered. "This is Chris, and we don't want to knock him over the first time that he's meeting you," she warned the excited dog.

It took her a little time as well as effort, but she did manage to calm down the German shepherd.

Finally, Lucy became quiet. "That's a good girl," Roe praised as she ruffled the dog's fur around her head and shoulders.

"I'm impressed," Chris told the vet, nodding his head in acknowledgment. "She actually listened to you."

"That's because she doesn't want to get me annoyed," Roe told him.

The rancher laughed to himself as his eyes swept over her. "I'll have to keep that in mind," he said.

"That's probably what she's thinking as well," Roe told him while petting the shepherd affectionately. Lucy moved her head into her mistress's hand, absorbing the vet's approval.

Chris pointed to the white ball of fluff moving

around them. "And who's this little guy?" the rancher asked Roe, scratching the small dog's head.

"This is Kingston," she told him. "He fancies himself to be the leader." Roe tried not to laugh as she made the introduction to the rancher.

Chris got a kick out of the declaration and laughed heartily. "There's nothing wrong with having illusions of grandeur." The rancher looked around slowly, taking the compact area in. "This is a really nice little place that you have here," he told her.

"Emphasis on the word 'little,'" Roe agreed with him with a laugh.

He got the feeling she'd taken his comment in a disparaging way. The way Christopher saw it, the living quarters were rather charming in their own unique way.

"You have to look at it in a positive light. That just means there's that much less for you to have to clean," the rancher pointed out with a grin.

"I had no idea that you had this optimistic way of looking at things," Roe commented. He certainly hadn't seemed that way, she thought.

"It's purely out of necessity," the rancher explained with a broad wink.

"Well, whatever the reason for it," she told him, "I think that Kingston highly approves of your optimism—and of you," she added as the little dog began dancing around the rancher again, trying his best to get the man to pet him and to show his approval. Roe flushed as the little dog continued leaping up at Chris to get his attention. "I'm really sorry about this," Roe apologized. "He's usually not *this* highly excitable. You seem to bring out an entirely different level out of him."

"Well, after spending so much time around sick cattle earlier, sharing a little time with this cute little puppy is certainly a refreshing change," the rancher told her.

He seemed to like both dogs, Roe thought, relieved to observe this about Chris. She had been afraid that all of Kingston's jumping up might annoy the rancher.

He was a really good guy, she thought. "Glad you feel that way, Chris. I didn't want you feeling that I was dragging you over here—or initially to attend the wedding rehearsal at the church," she added. She didn't want the rancher to feel as if she was forcing him to do anything.

"Trust me, you didn't drag me into anything," he told her. "I had a great time. Being here with your family—both at the church and at your grandfather's for dinner—was the most fun I've had since I bought the ranch from my brother." Sitting down on the sofa, he found himself wedged between both dogs, petting each one. They seemed to be competing for his attention.

She was curious about the circumstances behind the way he had come to own his ranch. "How did that work for you, anyway?" she asked him. "If you don't mind my asking, did your father favor your brother and leave the ranch to him and then you wound up buying it from him?" she asked. "I realize that it's none of my business, but—"

He held his hand up, stopping her. He had no problem telling her what went on. "No, my father actually left the ranch to both of us, but my brother didn't want to be involved in the ranch in any way. But truthfully, he wasn't about to have me take it over and run it for him. He made it clear he wanted no part of it and definitely didn't want to be tied down by it either. He wanted to walk away from it with money in his pocket, it didn't matter to him whose. So I took out a loan from the bank, and that way I was able to pay him off and he could go his own way."

He frowned a little as he related the tale to Roe. The only thing that made him smile a little was petting Kingston while he spoke.

"No gentleman's agreement between you and your brother, I take it?" she asked him sympathetically. She was beginning to see why he had taken to her family as readily as he had.

Chris laughed softly under his breath. "The only thing my older brother Pete ever had any sort of an agreement with was money. And why not?" he asked. "Money was the only thing that ever meant anything to my brother."

Leaning over, she petted Lucy who was still busy burrowing into Chris's hand. "I am so sorry to hear that, Chris."

"Don't be," he told Roe, dismissing her words. He

didn't want any pity. "I'm realistic about my family. My dad was a hard worker, but I knew the kind of person he was. In addition to being a hard worker, he was also a hard man to please. He had no patience for any of my mistakes. To be honest, I got the feeling that he liked Pete better. Pete was more like my father. I had no illusions that if I just did things the way he did, he'd suddenly see me through a set of brand-new eyes. He wouldn't and I knew he wouldn't.

"There was a reason why my mother didn't stick around," he confided. "My father wasn't a very likable man. He wasn't, for instance, anything at all like your grandfather."

She nodded. "Well, if it makes any difference to you, from what I hear, my father and Pop didn't exactly get along with each other either. As a matter of fact, my father had a huge fight with Pop. And when his mother, my grandmother, died, my father left home and enlisted in the army."

She sighed, remembering what her mother had told her. "The sad thing was that he and Pop never mended their fences. My father met and married my mother. She got pregnant and when she was close to giving birth, my father was away in the military and told her to come out here."

Roe smiled to herself, thinking about it. "My mother showed up on Pop's doorstep about to give birth to the three of us. Not long after, my father was killed in the war. He never did make up with Pop," she told Chris sadly. "Fences between my father and

Pop never got mended, but in spirit," Roe concluded, "and in his heart, Pop knew that they had been."

There was a loud crash of thunder just overhead. Roe quickly went over to the window and looked out. The rain was now coming down in sheets.

"You know, that doesn't look like it's going to let up soon. I think you should try to wait until it's not coming down so hard." She looked back over her shoulder at Chris. "Can I get you some coffee while you wait?"

"I wouldn't want to put you out," he said. "I all but exploded at your grandfather's home tonight. I don't need anything more to eat or drink. But if you don't mind, I'll just wait here until the worst of the storm passes."

She gestured toward the sofa, indicating that he should take a seat there. "Sure, I don't mind at all," she said.

Both dogs immediately raced over and sat down on the sofa. A laugh bubbled up to her lips. "I wasn't talking to you guys," she told the dogs.

Chris grinned, amused. "That's okay. They were here first, obviously before me."

She wasn't about to comment on that. Instead, she continued watching the rain. "You're welcome to stay here all night if it takes that long for the rain to let up. This isn't a big house, but it can accommodate me and a friend in the guest room comfortably enough."

His mouth curved in amusement as he nodded.

So he qualified as a "friend in the guest room," did he? "Why don't we wait and see what happens?" he suggested.

Roe returned the smile. "Fine with me," she told him.

Chapter Fourteen

Roe continued looking out the window, memories from her childhood crowding her mind. "You know, when I was a little girl, I used to love to watch the rain coming down. I could do it for hours and hours at a time."

"Well, with any luck that won't be happening tonight," Chris told her. "And even if it does go on raining hard, I can still go home. I'm not about to wind up washing away." He grinned as he came up to her. "The inside of my truck is pretty waterproof."

Roe's eyebrows drew together as she scrutinized him. She wasn't sure what he was trying to tell her. "Well, that's good to know." She tilted her head as she looked at him. "Is that your way of saying that you're ready to take your leave?"

"No, that wasn't my intention," he told her. "But I just didn't want to overstay my welcome."

Where had he gotten that idea? "That isn't about to happen for a very long while."

"Oh, good. That means I get to hang out with your pets some more," he told her, tongue-in-cheek.

"My pets and me," she corrected. "Unless this," she said, moving her hand around in a circle to include just Chris and her pets, "is intended to be a private party."

He looked at her for several seconds, and then, humor began to play on his lips. "It's whatever you want it to be," he told her.

Her eyes met his. It struck her for the umpteenth time that the man had to have just about the clearest blue eyes she had ever seen in a human being. Not just that, but those eyes seemed to look right into her, going straight into her very soul.

"Well, that could *definitely* be interpreted in a great many ways," she told him with conviction, smiling at the rancher.

She could have sworn that more than just a minor flash of electricity had passed between them. So much so that she could actually feel the electricity going from the rancher to her and then back again, lighting her up from within.

Not only that, but Roe was positive she could feel her very breath being stolen from her.

It took her more than a moment to be able to catch her breath as well as to regulate it. It took even longer than that in order to exercise the sort of control over it so that her pulse was no longer hammering wildly.

Breathing normally was becoming extremely tricky.

Standing so close to Chris, Roe found that she was extremely tempted to kiss the man. But at the same time, she did have her pride and she was not about to throw herself at the rancher, even if her lips were more than ready and eager to be planted on his.

She *really* needed to learn how to exercise control, Roe silently upbraided herself. No matter how tempting the man might be, she could *not* do anything about it. Restraint was the key word here.

"How *do* you want to interpret it?" Chris asked, looking at her.

"I'll let you know when I figure it out," Roe told him cavalierly, looking away so he wouldn't see her turning red.

At the exact moment that she looked away, Kingston bounced up behind her. The small dog managed to catch her off guard as he planted his small paws on her rear and pushed her. At the very same time, Lucy, her German shepherd, was pushing the rancher from his behind. What that accomplished was to not only close the gap between them but also create in one abrupt motion a movement that sealed Christopher and Roe to one another.

Caught completely by surprise, Roe gasped at the same time that Chris's mouth managed to come down on hers.

The contact that resulted was totally unplanned and at the same time, utterly memorable, causing her blood to heat as she felt sunshine race through her body.

She couldn't help thinking that the feeling was absolutely and utterly delicious.

When she could think.

Roe could feel her heart pounding wildly.

With her breath feeling as if it was solidly lodged in her lungs and her throat, Roe found herself clinging to the rancher as if her very life depended on it.

Her eyes widened as the wondrous sensation burrowed all through her, making her feel as if she was practically on fire. And then Roe closed her eyes, intent on absorbing what she was experiencing as well as just reveling in the absolutely wonderful sensation that was throbbing all through her like a wild, breathtaking drumroll.

Finding herself aching for him, Roe laced her arms around the rancher's neck, bringing her body even closer to his and delighting in the warmth generated between their bodies.

It never happened this fast, she caught herself thinking. She knew that. As a matter of fact, at least in her experience, it never really happened like this at all.

Roe couldn't remember *ever* responding to a man's touch or a man's kiss in this manner at all. The fact that she did took her completely and utterly by surprise, leaving her totally stunned.

And utterly, breathlessly mesmerized.

In the back of her mind, Roe knew that she should stop what she was doing, that she should draw the line before this whole thing got completely out of hand.

But heaven help her, she knew she really didn't want to stop.

Couldn't stop.

She had never felt like this about a man before, not in any manner, shape or form.

Granted, she had responded to Christopher years ago while they were still in high school. But in retrospect, that had been a subdued, controlled response, not this unimaginable, wild party thing that was going on inside of her. And heaven knew it hadn't been to this incredible magnitude that was going on inside of her right now.

She could barely catch her breath or get her wildly hammering pulse under control or even to slow down just a little.

And her pets were absolutely not cooperating, she realized. They were circling around her and Chris again, acting as if they were incredibly excited by what was going on.

It was as if the dogs could *feel* what was happening between them.

Roe was infinitely aware of the fact that she really did need to pull away, but somehow, no matter how much she silently lectured herself to do it, she just couldn't seem to get herself to act on it.

As a matter of fact, the exact opposite was happening and a deep, gnawing hunger seemed to be eating away at her.

And then suddenly, she felt Chris drawing his lips away from hers.

An almost frightening wave of sadness seized her heart and held it in its grip. Her breath caught in her throat and she stared at him, stunned.

Why was he pulling away? Did he find her that off-putting? Or was there some other reason for what was happening?

All sorts of questions popped up and multiplied in her head, but she forced herself not to say anything. She was ready to just walk away and hoped that she could do it before tears began spilling down her cheeks.

But when he spoke, the words that came from Christopher's lips completely took her by surprise.

He ran his hand along her cheek in a soft, slow, loving manner.

But his expression was nothing if not totally serious.

"I have a confession," he told her.

Roe could feel herself holding her breath. "And that is?" she asked in a low, hoarse voice.

"I realize that I have been in love with you for half my life," Chris admitted.

She stared at him, shocked. "Why didn't you say anything?"

"I didn't want to risk losing you."

Roe was completely speechless. Was he one of

those men who put women on a pedestal and if those women moved even so much as an inch in either direction, the men wound up losing interest?

"I don't understand," she told him, then repeated the words that surprised her more than anything else. "You've been in love with me for years?" she asked him incredulously. That alone was incredible, even more than his maintaining that it had been for half his life. She stared at him, hardly able to believe what he was telling her. "I never knew."

"You weren't supposed to know," he told her. "You were out of my league. You had a great family. You have one sister who helped the town during that devastating drought we experienced, another sister who's a nurse and you're a top-notch veterinarian. This while my family hardly stuck around to matter," he pointed out, then laughed at himself. "No wonder I have such a great relationship with animals. They're the only ones who ever mattered to me." He looked at her. "Except for you."

Roe ran the back of her hand along his cheek. "Are you planning on talking all night, or do you intend to do something else with your mouth?" she asked, her eyes gleaming as she looked at him.

Chris took her hand in his. "You never showed me where your bedroom is," he said.

Her mouth curved as she smiled at him. "No, I guess I didn't," she admitted. "My mistake." With that, she drew him along behind her. "It's right back here," she said, bringing him to it.

The bedroom was larger than he thought it would be. And a great deal more welcoming.

The moment they were inside her bedroom, Roe made a point of closing the door behind her, separating them from both of the dogs. Surprisingly, there was no barking. Neither dog registered too much displeasure over the event.

"Is it my imagination or did your dogs seem inclined to give us our space?" Christopher asked.

She smiled as, keeping her eyes on him, Roe began to unbutton his shirt.

"They're good little dogs," she told him as she began to tug his shirttails out of his waistband.

Christopher followed suit, tugging her jeans down her hips, managing to excite her as well as himself at the same time. His excitement grew and increased with every move he made.

Holding her against him, he began to kiss the nude woman in his arms over and over again, covering every square inch of her eager body. He succeeded in melting her from the inside out.

They had already taken off each other's clothing and in the process they managed to melt one another with each slow, measured movement they made.

She excited him beyond belief.

Roe felt the rancher's hands possessing her, molding her. Making her his. She moaned, absorbing the feel of his hands as they moved along her heated body. Her breath caught in her throat as she reveled in the way his hands moved along her flesh.

She had to bite her lower lip to keep from crying out. Roe knew she needed to keep her voice under control because if she made too much noise in response to the way he made her feel, the dogs might become excited and agitated, spurred on by the cries that were erupted from her lips.

So she took extra care as she slowly ran her hands lovingly along his bare flesh. In the process, she made herself as excited as she succeeded in making Chris.

And with each pass of his hands along her body, Roe could feel things happening, could feel the excitement growing larger and larger, mounting to huge proportions as it took steely root within her.

Switching positions for a moment, Roe rained a network of kisses down along his face and along his hard solid body, growing more and more excited as she did so.

Merging and moving along each other, they moved with an abandoned fervor on her double bed, enjoying each other to the fullest extent that they could.

They traded kisses and eager caresses as they tumbled about on her bed, absorbing the sensations they were generating within one another to the absolute extent that they could.

As Chris continued to forge a trail of small, sensuous kisses that feathered along the planes and slopes of her shoulders, exciting himself and her, Roe moved and rotated her body beneath his with a fervor that completely took his breath away.

Her body heated, growing increasingly hotter and hotter beneath his until she could barely stand it. Until she could barely breathe.

Her head was spinning wildly, making her more and more eager for his touch, for the taste of his mouth on hers. For every part of him.

Roe found herself trying her best to absorb him until such time as they could finally merge and become one.

Christopher anointed every part of her body with his lips, with his touch, until she wound up moving almost uncontrollably beneath him.

Her head spinning, she wrapped her limbs around his body.

Chris coaxed her back onto her back and forged a hot, moist trail all along her body. Roe could hardly contain herself as she wriggled and wiggled every part of her body against him, magnifying the fantastic effects she was experiencing along every single part of her body that Christopher brushed his lips against.

She could feel her whole body throbbing in utter anticipation for that final wonderful moment.

Roe was afraid she was breathing too hard for him to be able to hold her still.

Gathering her into his arms, he moved Roe until she was directly beneath him, and then he combed his fingers through her hair and cradled the back of her head.

He kissed her with every single ounce of feeling

he possessed just before he finally moved his knee in between her legs, parting them.

His eyes on hers, Chris slipped into her and then ever so slowly began to move. He moved more and more strongly within her.

And then, with ever-increasing rhythm he moved faster, matching Roe's every move until it felt as if they had been seized within the center of a giant hurricane, one that swirled them around this ever-growing sphere until, clinging to one another, they felt the explosion upon reaching the highest pinnacle.

An incredible euphoria swept over them, bringing them to the brink of ecstasy, making them experience the absolute height of everything that lovemaking had to offer—and more.

When it was over and Roe could feel herself slowly falling back to earth, she dug her fingers into his shoulders. She clung to him with every part of her being, breathing so hard she didn't think she would ever be able to catch her breath again.

She clung to Christopher for dear life until she was finally able to breathe normally.

Or at least something close to it.

Chapter Fifteen

The space next to her was empty.

The realization registered with Roe at the same time that her fingers swept around the empty space beside her. It was cold.

Chris was gone. It occurred to her that he had to have left more than just a few minutes ago.

Roe's eyes flew open as she sat up. An emptiness filled her as she simultaneously fought off a feeling of bereavement.

Instead of calling out for Chris—sensing there would be no answer—she looked around the bedroom.

There was no sign of him.

There were, however, her dogs. She remembered having closed the door when she and Chris came

into the room. Chris must have left the door opened when he left and her dogs had found their way in.

They had made their way onto the bed and appeared to now be sleeping. That was, until she opened her eyes and stirred. The moment she did, Lucy and her tiny fluffy partner in crime became exceedingly excited.

Frowning, Roe swept her hand under the covers and along the bed, just to be sure.

But it was cool.

Chris must have slipped out at least an hour ago while she was asleep. Sighing, Roe looked at the two pets.

"Hey, did you two chase him away?" she asked.

The expressions on the two dogs' faces looked as if they were actually trying to understand what she was asking them.

Roe laughed as she shook her head, dismissing the possibility. "No, I think you actually like him, which is good because with any luck at all, he'll be back." At least she seriously hoped so.

The two dogs snuggled up against her and for a moment, she allowed herself to enjoy the sensation. But then she forced herself to cut it short.

"Okay, time to start the day," Roe told her pets as she threw off her covers. Both dogs immediately scampered off the bed and then got out of her way. She looked down at the dogs. "Unless you want to get wet, I'd suggest you continue to stay out of my way for a little while longer."

Her pets all but tripped over one another as they vainly tried to move out of her way and to the side. Roe laughed affectionately as she made her way around the two dogs and went into the bathroom.

Moving as quickly as she could, Roe showered and was dressed even faster than usual. She knew if she slowed down, she would start to think and right now, she knew that thinking wasn't what she wanted to do.

Rushing around as she prepared to leave, Roe suddenly saw a folded note lying on top of her bureau. She instantly smiled as she realized the note had be from Chris.

Roe, the note read, *I didn't want to leave without saying goodbye, but I didn't want to wake you, either. Hope writing this note is okay. Last night was beyond anything I could have ever imagined, even in my wildest dreams. Funny how reality could turn out to be even better than your imagination. If I knew back then what I know now, I would have made my move on you a great deal sooner. Hope I was able to make you smile half as much as you made me smile,* the note concluded.

Roe sighed as she folded up the note. Then, holding the paper against her, she smiled. "You certainly managed to do that," she whispered to the handwritten piece of paper.

Looking down at the note, she couldn't help wondering where the rancher was able to find the paper.

It wasn't as if paper was readily accessible or even in sight.

She glanced toward the two dogs. They were looking at her as if she was imparting some sort of deep wisdom.

Roe looked at the paper and sighed with relief.

"Well, at least he didn't go running for the hills," she told the dogs with satisfaction. "If all of this goes well, who knows? He may wind up being your master, too.

"Who would have ever thought all those years ago back in high school we actually made a connection?" Roe said out loud. It certainly hadn't felt like it at the time.

Life was really strange, she decided.

She put out the dogs' bowls and was just about to leave the house when her cell phone suddenly rang. Taking the phone out, she glanced at the screen. Her heart skipped a beat when she saw the call was coming from Christopher.

Was he calling to apologize for leaving her side so abruptly, or was he calling her for some other reason?

"Answer the damn phone so you can stop guessing," she told herself sharply.

As she opened her cell phone, it occurred to her that maybe there was another reason for his call. Maybe something had gone wrong with his cattle. After all, this had all started with her coming over to his ranch to treat a few of his cows.

By the time Roe brought the phone to her ear,

her heart was pounding wildly and was now all but lodged firmly in her throat.

Instead of saying "Hello?" she asked almost breathlessly, "What's wrong?"

"What makes you think there's something wrong?" Chris asked her, clearly mystified by her assumption.

His question, worded the way it was, did not exactly inspire confidence in her.

"*Is* there something wrong?" Roe asked.

"Just that I had to leave your side this morning when all I really wanted to do was stay in bed and go on holding you in my arms." She heard the rancher sigh wistfully as he spoke. "Maybe someday," Chris concluded.

His voice was low and sultry and the sound of it created warm ripples of yearning all along her skin.

She told herself that she had to focus on the day ahead of her and stop daydreaming. However, she just couldn't convince herself that the man who had managed to light her fire had just called her for no reason.

"Are the cattle all right?" Roe pressed. She was, after all, a veterinarian first and the animals' welfare was her first concern.

"Amazingly enough," he told her brightly, "the cattle are all terrific. Rachel has bounced back exceedingly fast to the way she had been," he told her. "It was the most amazing thing to observe."

She could hear the smile in his voice. It was obvious he was deriving pleasure from the information he was imparting.

"That makes me very happy," Roe told him.

The rancher chuckled under his breath. "Well, I'm happy that you're happy," he told her, amused. And then his tone changed somewhat. "Well, I won't keep you. I just wanted to tell you that I had a really great time last night and that I'm looking forward to seeing you at the wedding this Saturday."

Roe smiled to herself at his declaration. "Count on it," she told him.

"I am," he responded and then told her, "Goodbye."

With that, reluctantly, the rancher forced himself to terminate the call he had made. Although he would have much rather remained on the line, just listening to the sound of her breathing, he knew he had a great deal of work to get to.

As did, he thought, the woman whom he had called.

Roe tucked her cell phone away. No time to daydream now. To begin with, she had a number of patients to look in on, patients she had already treated and patients she had promised to examine and diagnose.

This included examining one of her grandfather's horses.

It was going to be a very busy morning, and it promised to be an even busier afternoon.

Roe found herself really envying veterinarians

who only treated animals that could easily fit onto the space of a very small examination table instead of horses and cows and the like.

She saved her grandfather and his horse for late afternoon, knowing that Pop did get tired at that time, preferring to get most of his work done and out of the way in the morning hours.

So, after getting five patients under her belt, Roe drove to the ranch that she knew better than the back of her hand. Quite honestly, she would have preferred to ride in on a horse, but that would have taken her too much time. Driving a truck there was far more efficient, even though it wasn't nearly as much fun in her opinion.

"Hi, Pop," she called out as she pulled up in front, seeing the man inside the barn stall. "Did you put the patient up in the barn?" she asked.

Getting out of her truck, Roe walked up to her grandfather and quickly brushed her lips against the man's grizzled cheek.

"Uh-oh, someone didn't get as close a shave as he normally does," Roe remarked teasingly.

Her grandfather laughed it off. "They don't make razers like they used to. I take it that you're here to see Albert?"

"Well, I think the medical clinic would frown on my giving you an examination unless there was no way around it and you were in a very bad way, so yes, I am here to give your horse an examination." She circled around the stallion, petting his nose. "What did you say his problem was?"

"Other than having a vet who likes to crack wise?" her grandfather asked archly.

Roe smiled affectionately at the man. "Yes, Pop, other than having a vet who likes to make wisecracks."

Pop's expression turned serious as he regarded the stallion. "Albert seems to have developed a limp," her grandfather told her.

Roe nodded as she regarded her grandfather's stallion. "Okay, let's see what's going on with you, Albert," she said, taking her medical bag and walking into the stall.

"Slow down," her grandfather called out to her. "This isn't exactly a race, Roe."

"The sooner I take a look at Albert, the sooner I can get to the root of the problem and start to fix the poor little guy up," she said.

"Makes sense," her grandfather agreed, nodding his head. "As long as you're not inclined to conduct a foot race. By the way, how did last night go?"

Caught off guard by the question, Roe all but turned pale.

"What?" she cried, almost stuttering. She thought she must have heard him incorrectly. Her grandfather couldn't actually be asking her about last night—could he?

"Last night," her grandfather repeated. "You left here with Chris to show him your dogs. How did that wind up going? Did the dogs take to him?"

She practically breathed a sigh of relief at the way Pop had worded his question. For one uncertain moment, she thought her grandfather was referring to what had actually happened between her and the rancher.

She should have known better, she told herself. Pop would have never asked her anything even remotely as personal as that.

"It went very well, Pop. Lucy and Kingston took to Christopher immediately and Chris got a big kick out of them as well," she confided.

Roe didn't think she needed to say any more about her evening than that. Besides, Pop was a very clever, worldly man. He could easily put two and two together and wind up filling in the blanks more than adequately enough.

Pop sighed as he followed her into the barn.

"What's wrong, Pop?" she asked him as she set down her medical bag. She was preparing to do a slow examination of the leg that was obviously giving the horse trouble.

It took him a moment to put his feelings into words. "I'm going to miss you girls," he told her.

Roe furrowed her brow as she looked at her grandfather. "I don't understand," she said, confessing her confusion. "Raegan, Riley and I—and mom—are all right here."

"Yes, but you're not the little girls I'm used to having around. Raegan is married and Riley will be all too soon," he said with a sense of resignation.

"But I'm not," Roe pointed out as she slowly began her examination of the stallion, talking softly and slowly to the horse.

Her grandfather gave her a long, penetrating look that seemed to tell her he saw right through what she was telling him. "Aren't you?" he asked her.

"Pop, I don't even have anyone steady in my life, much less any sort of a pending relationship," she pointed out.

The expression on his face told her he knew better. "Things can change in a heartbeat," her grandfather said with the confidence of a man who had lived through a great many changes in his life.

"Well, right now my heartbeat is fixated on getting this guy up to par and walking better—and after that, I want to be able to make it through the wedding this weekend. After that," she said with a wide smile, "we can focus on marrying me off."

Mike smiled warmly at his technically last remaining unattached granddaughter as he held onto the young stallion, keeping it as still as he could so that she could work on the animal.

"Oh, I have no doubts about that at all," Mike told the girl he still thought of as "Rosemary" in his mind.

She wasn't sure what her grandfather was getting at, but for now she focused on the stallion she was treating and made no comment.

Roe was beginning to pack up her medical bag. For now, Pop's horse seemed to be on the path to recovery. Even his limp seemed a little bit better. She ran her hand along the horse's muzzle affectionately. "You gave us quite a scare, young man," she told the horse. "Glad you're on the mend." She looked at her grandfather. "He's going to be okay, Pop."

And then she paused, studying her grandfather. His face was drawn and his usual smile was missing. "But you're not," she observed. "Okay, out with it. What's wrong, Pop?"

"Nothing's wrong," he told her evasively, avoiding her eyes.

Roe put down her medical bag and faced her grandfather squarely. "One of the things I've always liked best about you, Pop, was that you didn't lie. Oh, you tried once or twice—or maybe even three times—but you could never really pull it off no matter how hard you tried. Now tell me, honestly, what's wrong?" she asked again. "And don't say 'nothing' because there clearly is 'something' wrong and I'd appreciate you telling me what it is, Pop."

Mike waved his hand at her question. "It's nothing to concern yourself about."

"Which of course is the best way to get me to worry," she said to her grandfather. "Look, I'm not about to leave until you level with me."

"I'll have Rosa get your old room ready," he told her cavalierly.

"Pop," Roe said to her grandfather in a warning voice. She was prepared to dig in until she got the truth out of him no matter how long it took.

Mike frowned. "You've got enough things to deal with without having this preying on your mind. Why don't we just forget about it?"

That was one thing she was unwilling to do. Roe sighed. "Pop, you are one of the most important people in my life and right now, you are really beginning to worry me. Now please, tell me, what's wrong? I'm not going to stop harping until you tell me," she told him, pinning him with a look. "You know I won't."

Mike sighed deeply, looking off over her head. "I miss your father."

She sensed there was something he wasn't telling her. "Why more today than any other day?"

His frown deepened. "Today marks the anniversary of the day your father left home." Mike waved his hand. "He just walked out and I never saw him again." Her grandfather turned to look at her. "That friend of yours, Christopher. There's something about him that reminds me of Ryan—of your father." He shrugged his shoulders, trying not to dwell on what he was saying. It still hurt. "Sorry, I didn't mean to be such a downer, honey," he apologized to his granddaughter.

"You're not a downer, Pop," she insisted. "What you are is human. I always suspected that you were. And now here you are, proving me right," she said, standing up on her toes and brushing her lips against his cheek. "Finally."

"Wise guy," he scoffed affectionately.

"Well, who made me that way?" she challenged with amusement.

He looked at her innocently. "I haven't the vaguest idea," he told her.

"Uh-huh. Well, I do," she said, her eyes meeting his. "Look, let me just put this into the truck and I'll come back to spend some time with you. We can talk."

"You don't need to babysit me, little girl," Pop told her.

"Maybe I want to," she told him. "Better yet, maybe I just need to talk to you. You were the one who taught me how important it was to share."

He repressed the smile that was trying to rise on his lips. "So this is my fault," he said.

Her eyes were shining as she said, "Uh-huh."

He laughed. "Okay, come to the kitchen. I think Rosa has some dessert lying around calling to us and needing to be consumed. We'll break bread and talk," he told her.

Her smile widened. "You had me at 'talk,'" she told him.

Mike paused for a moment. "I'm not keeping you from another patient, am I?"

"Pop," she assured him, walking with him to his house, "you can always keep me."

Chapter Sixteen

The following late afternoon Christopher was out with two of his wranglers. He was overseeing the cattle herd before it was time to bring them back and sequester them in the barn for the night when Jordan spoke up, calling to get his attention.

"Hey, don't look now, boss, but looks like you've got company." He pointed toward the approaching white truck they all recognized as belonging to the veterinarian. "There's nothing new wrong with the herd, is there?" the wrangler asked Chris.

The rancher turned his mount around in the direction that Jordan was indicating. "Not that I'm aware of," Chris answered.

The moment he saw Roe, the rancher could instantly feel his body coming to attention. Clicking his heels against the sides of his mount, Chris urged the mare over toward the approaching veterinarian's truck.

He leaned down from his horse, looking at Roe. "Hi, what are you doing here?" he asked her.

"And hello to you, too," she said cheerfully to the man who had brought new meaning to the word "intimacy" for her.

Chris had the good grace to flush just a little. "I didn't mean for it to sound that way," he apologized. "It's just that I didn't call you and we didn't have an appointment to meet out here this afternoon. Is there something wrong?"

He couldn't help wondering if Roe was having second thoughts about having him attend her sister's wedding with her. Had what happened between them the other night overwhelmed her?

Or had the lab called her with something further to be concerned about as far as the cow's bloodwork went?

All sorts of questions began popping up in his head.

Christopher stifled his sigh. Obviously running the ranch had definitely gotten him out of the habit of conducting any sort of an actual personal relationship.

But what Roe told him set his mind at ease now. "I had a little extra time so I thought I'd swing by and check in on my patient, make sure she hasn't had a relapse or anything along those lines," Roe explained. Her mouth curved a little as she got out of her truck, took out her black medical bag and closed the truck door behind her. "I didn't realize that I needed to make an appointment with you. By the way, there's no charge for a recheck," she told him in case the rancher was worried about that. Men's pride sometimes got in the way of thinking clearly about such matters, she thought.

Chris looked somewhat relieved. "Well, I appreciate that," he told her. "And I have to admit that I'm glad you were thinking about Rachel," the rancher confessed. "And in case I haven't made it clear, you certainly don't need to make an appointment with me ahead of time," the rancher assured her with a wide smile. "I didn't mean to make it sound like there was some sort of a procedure you needed to follow.

"To be honest," Chris continued, moving away from his men so he could have a more private conversation with the woman who had completely lit up his world, "I was thinking about this Saturday's wedding."

Roe couldn't read his expression and her mind instantly gravitated toward the worst possible thought. She could feel her heart turning to lead in her chest. "And you've decided not to go," she guessed.

That stopped him dead in his tracks. His question did her one better. "Have you changed your mind about inviting me to attend the wedding?"

She took in a breath before attempting to answer his question. "Do you want me to change my mind about it?" Roe countered, bracing for the worst. She did her best to explain what was behind her question. "I don't want you to feel like I'm putting pressure on you to attend the wedding ceremony if you really don't want to."

And then Christopher suddenly surprised her by laughing out loud at the question she had just put to him.

"What I feel like," he confessed in all sincerity, "is someone who suddenly finds himself stuck inside of a very strange comedy routine that doesn't seem to have an actual end in sight. Let me make one thing really clear to you, Roe. I am looking forward to going to your sister's wedding as long as you don't feel that I might wind up embarrassing you."

She stared at him as if he had just said something to her about preparing to sprout wings and wanting to fly around overhead at will.

What he had actually said made no sense to her at all.

Was there something dire going on that she didn't know about, or was this just Christopher's subtle way of trying to wiggle his way out of the invitation her grandfather had extended to him?

Or was she just misunderstanding things and everything was actually fine?

She was hoping for the latter.

"Okay," Roe allowed, "I'll bite. Exactly how would you embarrass me?"

"I don't know," the rancher admitted. "I'm just covering all the possibilities."

Okay, enough was enough, she thought, forging ahead. "Well, unless there's something that you're not telling me, or something that you're deliberately hiding about what you intend to do, there is *absolutely no reason* for me to feel embarrassed by you," she told the rancher in no uncertain terms.

Chris decided to go with the obvious, or at least what had struck him as obvious. It was minor, but it was an excuse. "My suit has seen better days," he said.

Roe got a kick out of his excuse and she laughed. "Chris, we've all seen better days," she said. "But as for your suit, if it's the one you wore when you attended the rehearsal, it looked fine to me. And before you ask," she said, holding up her hand to stop any comment from him, "no, no one else made a comment about it to me, or around me, snide or otherwise."

The rancher wasn't altogether sure he totally believed her. The conservative, dark blue suit had seen him through all sorts of occasions. That included graduation, both from high school and college, his father's funeral and any one of a number of other occasions that had come up in between those days.

"That suit has lasted through a great number of different occasions. And I did have it cleaned a number of times, but I think it's beginning to wear out," he confessed. "It won't be all that long before the material wears thin and I'll be forced to resort to having a tailor stitch it up."

She looked at him, totally unfazed by his excuse. "I'm pretty handy with a needle and thread. If you find that you need help mending something down the line, just ask me. I can take care of it for you," the animal doctor cheerfully volunteered.

Christopher looked at her in utter amazement. "You're serious?" he asked. "You can sew?"

Why would he think she was making this up? "Of course I'm serious. I can sew. I'm not a one-trick pony, you know. I can do a number of different things and one of them just happens to include sewing." And then she made a confession as to how this had all come about. "I didn't like waiting for my mother to get around to doing it for me. I have always preferred doing things for myself." She took a guess at what the rancher was thinking. "You know, sewing isn't something that's purely restricted to the soft and fluffy female of the species."

"I didn't mean to imply that it was," Chris told her. "If I did, I'm sorry. Okay, so do you want to take a look at Rachel to make sure for yourself that she's still doing well?"

Her broad smile answered his question.

"Lead the way," she told him, gesturing toward the building ahead of them. "I'll follow you to the barn."

Chris nodded his head. "Sounds good to me." Turning toward the two wranglers, he promised them, "I'll be back soon."

"Hey, don't hurry on our account, boss," Jordan told the rancher, grinning broadly. "We'll try to manage without you. It'll be rough," he confessed, attempting to keep a straight face as he said the words, "but somehow, we'll find a way to do it."

Chris made no answer. Instead, he followed the veterinarian into the barn.

Once inside, Roe concentrated on giving the cow a thorough examination. She wanted to make sure she hadn't missed anything the first time around and that nothing new had turned up in the last couple of days.

Chris kept quiet, not wanting to distract her until she was finished with her examination. He felt as if time was dribbling away in slow motion.

"Well?" Chris asked as he watched her retire her stethoscope into her medical bag and then snap it closed.

"Looks like Rachel is good as new," Roe declared, then amended, "Better even."

Christopher blew out a breath, then smiled broadly. "You have no idea how happy it makes me to hear that," he said.

A wide smile lit up her face. It seemed to go on for miles. "Oh, I think I can guess," Roe answered, and then the veterinarian sighed. She had put in a really long day and it wasn't anywhere near over. Time for her to get going, she decided.

"Well, if there isn't anything else you need me to do..."

His eyes lit up as he thought over her statement. "Oh, I wouldn't exactly say that," he told her, moving in front of her and blocking her way to her truck.

"For your animals," Roe interjected. Then repeated, "Anything more for your animals."

"Can you stay and talk a little while?" he asked. "It's almost time to get the herd back into the barn—or it will be in less than an hour," Christopher clarified, thinking that might be a way to entice her.

They were still in the barn, safely out of sight of his men. Still, she was not about to take any unnecessary chances and allow the two wranglers to witness any actions that might fuel speculation about what was going on between her and their boss.

Looking into his eyes, Roe slowly ran the palm of her hand along his cheek, caressing it but careful not to get caught up in the gesture. She didn't want to wind up involved in anything that might prove difficult to discontinue.

"I'm afraid I'm going to have to head back into town," she told him. She saw disappointment flash in his eyes which heartened her in its own way. She really wanted to mean something to the rancher. "I've got a lot to do before I can get ready for the wedding Saturday."

"Anything I can do to help?" the rancher offered instantly.

"Yes," she answered. "You can make sure that you'll be there." She pinned him with a look. "You will be there, right?"

His eyes met hers as he remembered what two nights ago had been like, spending it with this woman in his arms. He found himself really wanting to do it again.

And again.

"Right," he answered. "I promise."

She petted the cow she had been examining affectionately.

Observing her, the rancher could have sworn there was a bond of sorts forming between Roe and Rachel, the cow she had managed to cure.

Getting behind the veterinarian, Christopher whispered against her ear. "You know, I think she really likes you."

She wasn't about to argue the point or reject the supposition. Instead, she turned toward him and said, "I think all animals like me to a lesser or greater degree." And then she laughed, remembering an incident from her past. "I once scared my mother to death when I was a little girl. I managed to get this wild stray dog to come around by treating his injury. My mom thought he was rabid and would get me sick by biting me. She was trying to snatch me away, but I stubbornly refused. Eventually, I managed to treat him." She smiled, remembering. "He wound up getting better," she recalled proudly. "My mother barely recovered from that herself," she added with a laugh. "That poor woman went through an awful lot because of me when I was a kid."

"I'm sure that in hindsight, your mother recalls it all with a great deal of affection," the rancher said.

She laughed. "Yeah, now. Okay, I have dogs to feed at home and notes on the treatments that I've rendered today to transcribe. So I'll say my good-byes here and see you on Saturday, assuming your cow is all right and no symptoms show up between now and then."

"Does that mean I don't get to see you tomorrow?" he asked.

"If you don't, that'll make the day after tomorrow that much more special for me," she told him.

He laughed as he bent over and picked up her medical bag.

"You do have a very positive way of looking at things," Christopher told her. "I'll take this to your truck," he volunteered, waving for her to go on ahead of him.

Her independent way warred with what she took to be his sense of chivalry, but she was not about to get into any sort of a dispute with the rancher.

She didn't want anything being said that couldn't be unsaid.

Especially not so close to the wedding.

Her eyes washed over him and then she quickly brushed a kiss on his cheek. "See you," she told him.

He echoed her words back to her, accompanying them with a broad smile.

Chapter Seventeen

Roe spent a good deal of the following night tossing and turning. Try as she might, she just couldn't manage to get herself to fall asleep.

By five a.m. Roe gave up trying. Feeling somewhat nervous—"You would think I was the one getting married, not Riley," she murmured under her breath, Roe threw off her covers and padded off barefoot to the bathroom for a bath. Maybe that would make her feel more like herself.

She was being followed by a furry entourage.

Roe turned around to level a gaze at her two pets. "No," she told the two dogs making their way behind her, "you two stay out here. For once I want to take a leisurely bath. I think I've earned it," she said, shooing the dogs out of the small bathroom.

But even with the best of intentions, it just wasn't in Roe to take her time with a bath, although she did the best she could.

Ten minutes into it, she felt like a sloth. Her bath was over with rather quickly.

Riley might need her, she reasoned. If that turned out to be the case, she needed to get ready quickly, not dawdle, Roe told herself.

That being the case, she checked her cell phone both before and after she took a shower in preparation for the day that lay ahead.

When she came out of the bathroom a short time later, her pets ran to her, forming a tight, gleeful circle around her legs.

Roe laughed, pausing to pet first one dog, then the other. "You know something's up, don't you?" she asked, getting a kick out of the dogs. "I always said you guys were super smart."

With her bathrobe still wrapped tightly around her, Roe went into her bedroom and checked her maid of honor dress for possibly the umpteenth time in the last several days. Not that she had expected to have anyone break in and make off with the soft blue dress or anything of that extreme nature, she was more concerned about one of her pets accidentally getting its nails caught in the dress's material and ripping the fabric.

Roe knew that Riley had been waiting for this day to come since practically forever. More than anything, she wanted today to be perfect for her sister.

That meant absolutely everything involved in this big day needed to go well.

Roe saw the way her two pets were looking at her and interpreted their expressions in her own fashion. "I know, I know," she told the two dogs, "I worry too much. But I can't help it. I have never been the 'laid-back' type," she told them. She took her hair dryer out of the bottom bureau drawer and then closed the drawer with her foot. "I wish I was, but obviously wishing doesn't make it so," she said with a shrug.

She smiled ruefully, thinking about the fact that Riley had actually been in love with Matt for a very long time, thanks to being Breena's confidante and listening to her best friend talk about the man who had stolen her heart.

"Kind of like me and Christopher," she told her pets, "except that when I fell for him back in high school, at the time I had the feeling that he didn't even know I was alive."

Strange how things had a way of turning out, she thought to herself.

"Well, they're not going to wind up turning out at all if I keep dragging my feet like this," she told the reflection looking back at her in the mirror over the bureau.

As Roe slowly and meticulously began getting dressed, she realized she and Chris had made no actual final arrangements about his coming to pick her up—or even at what time he intended to show up on her doorstep.

For all she knew, the rancher was planning to meet her at the church.

How could she have been so lax, she silently upbraided herself.

This was what happened when she had little to no experience when it came to dating, she silently lectured. If she had had the proper experience, she would have made the right arrangements.

Well, she was going to need to fix that—as soon as she got dressed.

Very carefully, Roe slipped on the light blue dress, being very careful not to snag or pull the material. Once the dress was on, she looked herself over in the mirror. She didn't have a vain bone in her body, but she smiled, pleased by what she saw.

"Not bad," she observed, looking herself over from every single angle she was able to see.

She began looking for her phone to call Chris when it suddenly rang.

She fervently prayed the call wasn't from someone looking for a veterinarian to treat their pet. Not today. But she doubted there was an actual real danger of that. Forever was a small town and almost everyone knew everyone else's business.

In this case, the people in town all knew that one of the triplets was getting married today and that the entire family was going to be there for the occasion. That meant no one was going to be calling her unless there was a life or death emergency.

She picked up the phone. "Hello?"

"Roe?"

She felt her heart skip a beat. It was as if she had willed this call from Christopher to happen. She had to refrain from breathing a sigh of relief. "Chris, what can I do for you?" she asked the rancher.

"I hope I'm not waking you up," he told her.

"No, I've been up for a while now," she told him. She wasn't about to mention that she hadn't been able to get to sleep last night.

"I figured that," he admitted. His voice was low and sultry and so incredibly sexy. "I was just wondering what time you'd like me to come over. We didn't discuss this the other day, but I thought that since we're going to the church together, I should pick you up. And before you say anything," he went on, "I can come by as early as you'd like. Now, if it suits you." And then he stopped himself. "Unless you made plans to go to the church with someone else."

Why would he say that, she wondered. "You make it sound like I'm playing games. I just want you to know that I'm not in the habit of doing things like that. I never have been," she told him firmly.

Chris backtracked quickly. "I didn't mean to imply I thought that's what you were doing." Taking a breath, he tried again. "I think I'm trying so hard to make you understand that I'm being straightforward with you that I'm tripping over my own tongue."

Roe felt bad. "You know what? I think we're both nervous. Which means we're both tripping over our own tongues. Let me start over," she told him.

"You're welcome to come by any time, Chris. I'm all dressed and ready to go. I have been for the last half hour," she confessed. Then she added, "I guess you might say that I'm anxious about this wedding. I couldn't get any sleep. So if I start wilting in your arms while we're dancing, I'd take it as a personal favor if you would find it in your heart to drag me around the floor so no one realizes that I'm sinking."

She didn't know how he might take that. She wasn't sure what to expect. She certainly hadn't expected him to start laughing, but he did.

When he was finally able to talk again, he told her, "Well, I'll do my best. Since you're ready, I can be there in about forty-five minutes."

"I'll be here," she promised, then added, "Waiting."

He could hear the smile in her voice.

The promise of her waiting for him got his blood going in anticipation.

"Anything you need me to bring?" he asked.

"Just yourself," she told him in complete seriousness.

"Now I can certainly do that," he answered. "Okay, see you in less than an hour," Chris promised.

And with that, the rancher ended the call.

Roe tucked her phone away into the small purse she was planning to bring with her and then looked at her pets. "Well, he's coming over, guys. It would be great if you didn't jump all over him when he gets here."

Lucy tilted her head at her as if she was attempting to understand what was being said. Kingston followed suit. Roe smiled at them, certain that her pets understood her perfectly.

"Don't play dumb," she told the two dogs. "I know you understand every word I say to you. I stopped being taken in by your little act a long time ago." She bent down so that they could hear her better. "Now I want you to listen to me very carefully. Christopher Parnell is very important to me. He has been for many years now. You guys are smart enough to sense that," she told the dogs. "I don't want you messing this up or scaring him off with your behavior, understand?" she asked. She could have sworn the pets looked as if they were taking all this extremely seriously. "Okay, as long as we understand each other and you're nice to him, everything is going to be all right between us"

Moving around the small house, Roe did a quick, last-minute check, making sure that everything was as neat and tidy as it could be.

Although the rancher didn't strike her as a picky person, she still didn't want to create a bad impression on the man, especially since she wasn't a messy person by nature. Sometimes, though, things did have a tendency to get away from her.

Giving both her house and herself a last, thorough once-over, Roe got her gift ready for the newlyweds to take with her and then waited for Chris to arrive.

* * *

It took the rancher longer to get to her house in town than she had expected. He probably had trouble getting out on time, she guessed.

The moment Chris rang her doorbell, she was at the door, throwing it open.

"The dogs have been waiting to say 'hi,'" she told him with a grin.

He smiled at her pets. They came at him eagerly. "Hi, guys," he said, greeting them.

Turning, Chris gave Roe a very quick kiss on the lips. He wanted the kiss to be longer, but he knew if he gave in to the urge that was drumming through him, they might never make it out the door on time, and they did have a wedding to get to.

"Are you ready?" he asked her. "I thought we might take my truck since you're always using yours for business purposes." His eyes met hers. "I hope I'm not usurping you. I mean, if you'd rather take your truck, I've got no problem with that. I just thought this way might prove to be a better, more economical choice for you."

"Your truck will be fine," she told him, smiling. And then she turned to look at her pets. Just before Chris arrived, she had put out their food. She hadn't wanted them stuffing themselves too soon.

"I'll see you guys late tonight," she promised.

The dogs yipped and accompanied the two humans to the door. They stood obediently to the side as their mistress and her friend left the house and closed the door behind them.

She noticed that Christopher's truck had been freshly washed and she remarked on it.

He grinned, pleased that she noticed. "I thought that maybe I'd wind up convincing you to take my truck, and if I did, I thought it should be clean for the occasion," he told her, smiling. "So I washed it. I actually like having a clean truck. It's just that between the ranch and taking care of the cattle, things tend to get away from me. I have no idea how people with larger ranches manage to get things done," he admitted. "Never mind large families."

"They tell me it gets easier over time," she told him, thinking of her grandfather. "That, and you wind up hiring more wranglers to come and help you out with the work when you need it."

"Yeah, provided you have the money," Chris remarked. He had yet to turn a decent profit to be able to afford more than the wranglers he already had.

"You could always breed your cattle," she pointed out. "Having large numbers can really provide money."

He shrugged off the solution. "Maybe someday," he murmured. "By the way, have I told you that you look beautiful in that dress?"

"No, but you can," she said, fighting to suppress a grin. "A woman never tires of hearing that she looks good in something."

"Not good," he corrected. "Beautiful. I'm very

happy that I found the time to clean my truck. I wouldn't have wanted you to risk getting that beautiful dress of yours dirty."

"That's very thoughtful of you," she said. "Although if there was a problem with your truck being dirty, I could have always sat on a blanket or gotten a sheet from my linen closet to sit on. I don't really require much and I'm not generally a messy person, especially not when so much preparation went into getting ready."

"I'll keep that in mind," he said, winking at her. "If it wouldn't mess your makeup, I'd kiss you."

She looked at him in complete innocence and told him seriously, "Makeup can always be touched up or reapplied later."

Chris took that as an invitation. Stopping the truck, he pulled Roe into his arms, inclined his head toward her face and pressed his lips against hers.

Roe melted into his kiss just long enough to enjoy it—and then pulled away.

When he looked at her in surprise, she whispered, "Later."

The rancher took that to be a promise and kept it close to his heart.

Chapter Eighteen

The moment Chris had leaned in closer, even before his lips had a chance to touch hers, Roe could feel her pulse surging.

Could definitely feel herself melting.

Her eyes smiled up into his. "The maid of honor has to be able to walk," she whispered to him. "And you are making that very, very difficult."

Chris exhaled as he drew back.

"Sorry," he apologized. "I got carried away and you do have a point. You do need to be able to walk. It's just that I can't seem to be able to resist you. It's not an excuse," he told her. "It's just a given. After all these years, I've finally come to my senses and it opened my eyes." He flushed a little. "I suppose that part of me is trying to make up for lost time."

He straightened out in his seat. "I'm sorry. I didn't mean to come on so strong."

Oh lord, the man was really warming her heart, Roe couldn't help thinking. "I wasn't trying to take you to task. It's just that we have a wedding to attend. A wedding that I can't be late to because my sisters will kill me. Not only that, but a little girl will be heartbroken and my grandfather will take me to task like it's nobody's business."

Chris started up his truck and put it into gear again. It occurred to him that she hadn't said anything about one member of her family in all this.

"What about your mother?" he asked. "How would she react?"

Roe's smile widened. "I'm really blessed in that department. My mother would forgive me for doing just about anything," she told him, then amended her words to say, "Everything, actually."

The rancher grinned as he drove. "I knew I really liked that lady. And although it's tempting," he continued, sparing her a glance, "I'm not about to give in to my urges. It also wouldn't be very mature. However, if you're not doing anything *after* this wedding is all wrapped up and put to bed, I'd like to do the same thing with you."

"That sound like an offer I shouldn't refuse," she said with a wide smile.

"I'll hold you to that," Chris promised.

"I'd like that," Roe said with a wide smile.

A few minutes later, the rancher pulled his vehicle

into the church's parking lot. It was still rather early as far as the wedding service was concerned, but there were already a few vehicles parked in the lot.

As she got out of Chris's truck, Roe recognized her grandfather's car and a couple other cars that were in the lot.

"I think Pop brought the bride and Mom to the church," she told the rancher. Roe's smile widened as she turned toward Chris. A sparkle came into her eyes. "It's really happening."

Roe had managed to lose him. He was unclear as to what she was referring to. "What is really happening?" he asked her.

Raising the hem of her dress, Roe carefully navigated the steps leading into the church. Chris took hold of her arm to make sure she didn't trip on the gown's hem.

"Riley is finally marrying the man she has secretly been in love with for years," she said.

"Years?" the rancher questioned. Holding the door open for her, Chris escorted Roe into the church.

"Well, ever since Matt came out here to spend the summer and he and Breena wound up falling in love with each other. But then he had to go home for school. When Breena found herself pregnant, she made sure there were barriers up between her and Matt, even though she still went on loving him.

"Listening to the stories that Breena had to relate, Riley found herself falling in love with him by proxy. According to what Riley had to say, she didn't even know it was happening *while* it was happening," she told the rancher with a grin.

He nodded his head, looking rather serious and interested in what she was relating. "Once these vows are exchanged," he nodded toward the church, "I'd really like more details."

Roe's smile widened. This was quickly becoming her favorite story. "I'll be more than happy to give you those details," she told him as they entered the church. "But right now..."

He nodded, not needing any more than that. "I know. We have a wedding to attend."

She beamed at him. After caring about the man for so long, she could hardly believe they were actually here together for this occasion.

Her eyes were shining. "Exactly," she agreed. Slipping her arm through his, she gave him a soul-melting smile. "Let's go."

The moment her grandfather and mother saw them, they both smiled.

"You made it," her grandfather declared, looking directly at Roe.

Roe looked at the older man in surprise. "Of course, we made it. Why would you think we wouldn't?"

"Pop sometimes has a tendency to think the worst," her mother said matter-of-factly for Christopher's benefit.

"But you don't?" Chris asked genially.

Dressed in a floor-length gown that was a darker shade of blue than the bridesmaid dresses, Rita turned toward the young man standing beside her last unattached triplet and smiled.

"I drove out here when I was nine months pregnant with triplets. I came all the way from the East Coast. If I could do that, then nothing can really daunt me," she informed the young rancher.

Chris smiled at Roe's mother. "That is pretty impressive," he agreed.

Roe glanced at her watch. "We've got an hour until the wedding starts," she announced to her grandfather and mother. "Do you need me to do anything for you in preparation?"

Rita touched Roe's face affectionately. "Just be here," she answered.

"How about me, Mrs. R?" Chris asked. "Can I help with anything?"

"Now that you mention it, we could use a few more ushers escorting the guests into the church pews," she told the young man.

Rita almost added that it would be good practice for him but decided it might be better not to say anything like that at this point. There was no sense in scaring the young man before he popped the question to Roe, something she was completely convinced he would do, given enough time.

She caught her father-in-law looking at her and knew that he felt the same way she did. She moved closer to Mike.

"I really wish Ryan was here," she told the older man softly.

"He is, Rita," Pop told her in a low voice, glancing in Roe's direction. "He is."

"What are you two whispering about?" Roe asked them, moving closer to them.

"That it's time to start getting everyone into proper positions," Pop told Roe innocently.

"Are Riley and Raegan here already?" Roe asked her grandfather. Now that she thought about it, she didn't remember seeing their vehicles in the parking lot, although she hadn't really looked around for them at the time.

Her grandfather chuckled as if this was an inside joke.

"You know you're always the last one to arrive, Roe," he told her. He glanced at the young man who had brought her. "She is, you know. Roe has many wonderful qualities, but being early was never one of them."

"Pop, don't you have any instructions you'd like to share with the priest?" Roe asked her grandfather innocently, attempting to distract him. "Because if you do, he's right over there." She pointed to him standing in the front of the church by the lit candles.

"See what I mean?" Mike asked Chris. "Roe never lets up. That's a really handy trait to have as a veterinarian and when you're working out a problem or trying to finish a task, but not so much when you're having a dispute with her."

The rancher smiled at the woman next to him.

"So far," he confided to Roe's grandfather, "that really hasn't come up."

"Well, you boys can go on chewing the fat all you want, but I have to go find my sister and let her know I'm here to back her up on her big day. Mom?" she asked, turning toward her mother.

"Just waiting for you to say the word, darling," Rita told Roe just before she led her away.

"Come with me, boy," Mike told the rancher, taking him off in another direction.

Roe watched the two men disappear around a corner, wondering if she should be concerned. Her mother was leading her down the corridor.

"Have I told you girls how proud you've all made me?" Rita asked as she brought Roe into the small room where Raegan, Riley and Vikki were getting ready for the ceremony.

Roe nodded at her sisters and her niece as she walked into the room. "Not in the last forty-eight hours," she answered her mother.

"Be nice to her, Roe. This is hard on Mom. She doesn't like crying and she always winds up crying at weddings," Raegan told her sister.

"Especially our weddings," Riley noted.

Vikki looked confused. "Why does she cry at your weddings?" she asked, looking from Riley to her grandmother-to-be. "Doesn't she like going to your weddings?"

"It's something that happens when people get

older," Riley told her. She ruffled Vikki's hair. "You'll find out all in due time, sweetheart."

"Not me," Vikki told her in utter seriousness.

"And why is that?" Rita asked, struggling not to grin at Vikki's serious expression.

"Because I'm never getting married. It's too much work," the little girl declared.

"I'll remind you that you said that in a few years," Roe told the little girl. And then she turned toward the bride-to-be. "Want me to pin your hair up?"

"Is that your way of saying that I look messy?" Riley asked.

"No, that's my way of remembering that you like to wear your hair up on special occasions and I'm offering to do it for you. If you'd rather wear it down, go right ahead," Roe told her genially. "You look lovely that way, too."

Raegan smiled as she turned toward the bride-to-be. "Our Roe has gotten more diplomatic since my wedding."

"Thank heaven for small favors," Riley murmured. She gestured toward the bureau. "You'll find everything you need in there, Roe. I had the presence of mind to bring it along with me when I left the house this morning."

"And when you finish doing her hair," Vikki nodded toward Riley, "could you do mine, too?" she asked hopefully.

"Absolutely," Roe answered the little girl with a broad wink.

Vikki clapped her hands together joyfully and jumped up and down. “I knew you would.”

Roe paused to kiss Vikki’s forehead.

“Better get to it,” Raegan prompted, glancing at her watch. “You don’t have that much time before the ceremony starts.”

“No problem.” Roe gestured toward a chair. “Sit,” she prompted. “Nervous?” she asked as she got started combing Riley’s hair.

“Only that you might wind up making me look like the Bride of Frankenstein,” Riley quipped.

Roe’s eyes met Riley’s in the mirror. “I promise I won’t.”

“Who’s that?” Vikki asked. “Frank-y-stein.”

“Nobody for you to worry about, Little One,” Roe assured the girl as she got to work on Riley’s hair.

Within minutes, Riley had her sister’s hair completely swept up and piled high on her head.

“You look beautiful,” Vikki told her future mother in awe.

Riley’s eyes crinkled as she turned toward the little girl. “You couldn’t have said anything nicer to me.”

Grinning, Vikki swung around toward Roe. “Now do me! Do me!” she prompted eagerly.

“Your word is my command, Your Majesty,” Roe said, gesturing for Vikki to sit down on the edge of the bed.

Vikki wriggled into place, doing her best to be patient, although it obviously wasn’t easy for the little girl.

Roe gently secured a towel around Vikki's neck. Making sure that it wasn't on too tight, the maid of honor got to work.

Chapter Nineteen

Roe had just finished putting her sister's and Vikki's hair up when, in the distance, she heard the familiar strains of the wedding march beginning to play. Within seconds of that, there was a knock on the dressing room door.

"Okay to come in?" a deep voice on the other side of the door asked.

"We're all decent in here, Pop," Roe called back.

Her grandfather opened the door and peeked in. "I never had a doubt." He raised his hand in front of his eyes as if to shield them. "I should have worn my sunglasses. All this beauty in one place is just too much for me to handle."

Coming into the room directly behind her father-in-law, the girls' mother laughed.

"Oh, I'm sure you'll manage, Pop," she told him, then looked at Riley. There had been a few last-minute changes in the wedding gown, including the addition of more lace. Rita thought the resulting gown looked compelling. "You look breathtakingly beautiful, Sweetheart." Rita's smile swept over all three of her daughters. "You all do, girls."

"Even me?" Vikki asked.

Rita hugged the little girl to her chest, secretly wishing that Vikki's mother could be here to see this. She didn't dwell on the complications that might arise if that happened.

"Especially you, Little One," she told her.

Mike looked at Riley as the organ music grew louder and more powerful. "They're playing your song, honey," he told the bride.

Presenting his arm to Riley, Mike Robertson led his granddaughter off into the church proper.

"All right, let's go, girls. Mrs. Abernathy gets tired quickly," their mother said, referring to the organist playing the wedding march.

Vikki obediently scampered quickly out of the room, following Riley and the man who was about to officially become her great-grandfather.

Everyone inside the church turned in unison the moment the entire wedding party entered the church. Appreciative murmurs rose, filling the air.

For his part, Chris's eyes were exclusively on Roe, who was slowly making her way down the aisle ahead of Riley and their grandfather. She was following Raegan and her husband, Alan. Matt had asked Alan to be his best man.

Chris was very aware of the fact that all three sisters, being triplets, looked alike. Yet in his eyes, Roe was the most beautiful of the trio.

Beautiful enough, to take his breath away.

The entire ceremony seemed to be unfolding in slow motion to him—except for when Vikki came in, mightily scattering rose petals all along the church's carpet, from the doorway to the altar.

Standing up in the front pew, Rita smiled at the look on the little girl's face. Vikki looked very proud of herself, as if every bunch of rose petals she threw had been aimed and successfully thrown. Vikki was beaming by the time she finished.

When the wedding party had positioned itself, Father Lawrence began speaking the words that everyone was waiting to hear. "Dearly beloved..."

Twenty-five minutes later, Father Lawrence ended the ceremony by declaring, "I now pronounce you husband and wife." Then, when he added, "You may now kiss the bride," cheers and applause went up like a warming wall of noise all around the wedding party and the church itself.

Mike exchanged glances with his daughter-in-law, as if silently proclaiming, "Two down, one to go."

Nodding her head, Rita's smile widened as if she was happily agreeing with her father-in-law.

More cheers and applause filled the church as everyone converged around the newly married couple.

Vikki was jumping up and down and applauding and cheering louder than anyone.

Everyone eventually filed out of the church and moved on to the bar, Murphy's, that was run by Brett, Finn and Liam, the three Murphy brothers. It had been agreed that the celebration would be held there. The family-owned establishment had been reorganized in order to handle the food from Miss Joan's diner that had been prepared for the occasion, along with the refreshments that the bar normally served.

"I'd forgotten about this place," Chris admitted as he walked Roe into the brightly lit establishment. "I had my high school graduation here and then left the next day for college…until I had to come back when my dad had his heart attack," he added quietly.

Roe looked at him. "No sad memories today," she told the rancher. "Today is for celebrating and for making good memories for the future."

Chris saw no reason to dispute that. He nodded his head. "You're absolutely right," he agreed, smiling at the woman who filled his dreams.

Liam, the youngest of the three Murphy brothers, along with his band, played music to accompany the wedding party and everyone celebrating with them as they entered the establishment.

The moment he heard the music, Chris looked at the maid of honor. "May I have this dance?" he asked.

She smiled brightly at him, giving him her answer before she said a single word. "I thought you'd never ask."

He grinned at her. Chris was not about to tell Roe that it had taken him all this time to work up his nerve to ask for this dance. Instead, now that she had agreed, he happily took her hand in his, put his other hand on her waist and began to dance.

After just a few moments, Roe looked up at him and smiled. "I had no idea you were such a good dancer," she told him.

"There're a lot of things about me that you don't know," Chris told her seriously. "There's a lot about me *I* don't know," he admitted with a chuckle as he looked into her eyes. The music went on playing, seemingly surrounding them.

They, along with a number of other people, went on dancing for a good forty-five minutes as one song melded into another.

At that point, Miss Joan decided it was time to serve the food.

"Time to sit down, folks, and rebuild your strength," the woman informed them.

It wasn't a suggestion, but more of a direct order. One that the people of Forever knew better than to ignore.

So, one by one, the couples left the makeshift dance floor the Murphy brothers had created and took their places at the surrounding tables, waiting for Miss Joan's servers to make their rounds.

Miss Joan was moving solicitously around the

tables, making sure everyone who was seated had been served.

It was as if, for now, Miss Joan was symbolically their mother and everyone who was seated were her children. It didn't matter that she was a good deal older than most of them were.

"Eat," Miss Joan said gruffly to the few who had demurred at having their plates piled high with food. Miss Joan firmly believed that everyone needed to consume a healthy amount of food.

"I might have to be surgically cut out of my wedding dress," Riley complained when she finished consuming her meal.

Raegan shot the bride a warning look. "That can't happen until Roe has her turn using it." It was clear that she assumed Roe would be wearing the dress next rather than purchasing her own.

"Don't worry about me," Roe warned. "That might be years in coming—if it comes at all."

"Oh, it'll come," Mike said with confidence as he signaled the server to bring him a second serving of chicken. He turned his attention toward Miss Joan, who was still making the rounds. He pointed to the food on his plate. "This is really good," he told the older woman. "My compliments to whoever put this all together for us."

Miss Joan offered the man a small, albeit pleased smile. "I'll pass that word along," she told the bride's grandfather. She lingered at their section of the table for a bit, looking at the bride. An almost sentimental expression came over the woman's face. "You know, I can remember the night I helped bring those three into the world—and now look at them," she declared, gesturing at the trio. "Who would have ever thunk it?" she asked, looking at the girls. What passed for a smile was on the woman's thin lips.

"Me," Mike answered. "I never doubted it, not for even a second," he told the older woman.

Miss Joan gave the man what could have passed as a warm smile.

Chris leaned in toward Roe and asked in a low voice, "Do you think you're able to dance, or would you want to sit and wait a while longer?"

Roe had a feeling that if she waited even for a little longer to get up from the table, her grandfather might take the opportunity to find out if she had any plans that might include getting married in the immediate future. She knew it had to be on his mind, and she had no way of knowing what Christopher might answer in that case. Dancing, even if she felt full, might be the better way to go, she decided.

"Oh, I think that it's safe enough to risk taking to the dance floor at this point," she told Chris.

"Good, because I don't know about you, but if I eat any more, I'm probably going to wind up exploding," he confessed. "So dancing is a good diversion right now."

* * *

Not long after that, Roe felt as if she was very close to dancing her feet off.

In reality, from the time they had left her house until right now, a total of seven hours had gone by. Wedding guests were beginning to leave the Murphys' bar and go home.

Riley and Matt had already left and gone off on their honeymoon. They had left a very sleepy Vikki with Rita and her father-in-law.

"I think this young lady needs to be put to bed," Pop declared quietly. He began to rise, preparing to carry the little girl to his car.

But before he could get up, Chris was on his feet beside him. "Let me carry her to the car for you, sir," the rancher offered.

Mike gave him an inscrutable look. "Are you saying I'm old, boy?"

"No, I'm saying that maybe all that celebrating made you somewhat tired—a bit too tired to carry your new great-granddaughter to the car," he elaborated. And then he smiled at the man. "No offense intended. I'm just trying to help, sir."

"And he's just trying to bust your chops, Christopher," Rita told the rancher with a wide smile. "In his own endearing way, of course," the man's daughter-in-law added by way of an explanation.

"There she goes again, giving away all my secrets," Mike said, pretending to complain, shaking his head. "All right, tell you what. You can take this little princess and put her into her car seat. I'll lead the way. Rita?" he asked. "Are you ready to go?"

"Always," the woman answered cheerfully. She looked at her two remaining daughters at the table. "See you for Sunday dinner," she told them as well as her son-in-law. As far as she and Mike were concerned, unless there was some sort of state of emergency, Sunday dinner with the family was a given.

"Yes, Mom," Roe and Raegan echoed in unison before their mother left the table and walked a short distance behind her father-in-law.

The next moment, Roe was on her feet as well, following behind the twosome and the sleeping child that Chris was carrying.

"I'd better go after them. Chris might forget he brought me," she quipped.

"Fat chance of that happening," Raegan said with a laugh. "I saw the way he looked at you today. He'd sooner forget to breathe than he'd forget that he brought you to the wedding."

"I have no idea what you're talking about," Roe said to her sister, feigning innocence.

"I can explain it to you," Raegan offered cheerfully, her eyes gleaming.

"Maybe some other time," Roe answered, throwing her words over her shoulder.

Grabbing her purse and her wrap, Roe hurried out the door and into the parking lot.

She got there just in time to see Christopher tucking Vikki into her car seat in the back of Pop's vehicle. She was impressed that he looked as if he knew what he was doing.

Finished, Chris stepped back, allowing her mother as well as grandfather to take their places within the car.

"Thank you, dear," Rita said to Christopher. "He won't admit it, but his back has been giving him some trouble lately."

Mike gave his daughter-in-law a disgruntled look. "I won't admit it because it's not giving me any trouble," he maintained. "My daughter-in-law is given to having these wild flights of fancy at times. But I do thank you," he told Chris. "That was very nice of you. Although she doesn't look it, that little girl likes to eat her weight in dessert and food practically daily," he confided to Chris. After buckling up, he put his key into the ignition. "Ready?" he asked, looking at his daughter-in-law.

"Ready," she told him with a smile.

Mike started the car and within moments, they were on their way out of the parking lot and off to the ranch.

Chris turned toward Roe. "Are you ready to go home?" he asked her.

"Whose home?" she asked him pointedly. "Your home or mine?"

He paused to look at her. "That choice is totally up to you,"

"Mine," she said without any hesitation. She didn't want to take a chance on any of his men seeing her coming over to his house at this hour. Besides, she waned to feed the dogs in the morning.

The rancher smiled at her, his eyes crinkling. "Yours it is," he agreed just before he started up his vehicle.

Roe sat back in the passenger seat, totally pleased and content as she allowed herself to contemplate the evening that lay ahead of her.

Chapter Twenty

The moment that Roe and Chris walked into the veterinarian's house, Kingston and Lucy came racing up to greet them. The pets seemed to be lying in wait at the door's threshold and were obviously excited about their appearance the moment they walked in.

The dogs were running around the duo at what seemed like top speed.

"Okay, guys," Roe told the dogs, "back off. Chris and I have put in an extremely long day at the ceremony and Chris is mine tonight." Out of the corner of her eye, she caught the rather pleased, amused expression on the rancher's face. She turned toward him. "I didn't mean to make you laugh."

"I'm not laughing," Chris protested innocently. "This just happens to be my really, really pleased look."

"Then I take it you're not too tired?" she asked, looking at him, her voice drifting off as she left the rest of her question unsaid.

Christopher's eyes met hers. He knew exactly what she was referring to.

"Too tired?" His smile grew wider and deeper. "For that to happen, I would have to be dead," he told her, his meaning very clear.

Roe placed her hand on his chest and was completely captivated by the way his heart was pounding. "Well, you're certainly not dead," she happily informed him.

As he allowed himself to be led off by her, Chris took note of the fact that Roe's pets were following right behind them. He paused by the entrance to Roe's bedroom. "Sorry, guys, you have to stay out here," he told the dogs. "Maybe you can come in later. That's all up to your mistress," he said, smiling as he looked pointedly at the veterinarian.

"You heard the man, guys. I get him first," she told her two pets.

With that, Roe slipped into the bedroom with Chris following directly behind her.

He closed the door behind them.

The moment it was closed, Chris took her into his arms and brought his lips down to hers. He kissed her soundly and with every fiber in his being.

And then, with his heart pounding madly, he forced himself to draw his lips away from hers.

"I have to admit that I've been thinking about

doing that all day," he told her. "As a matter of fact, I've been thinking about doing that ever since we first made love—and even before then," he admitted, threading his fingers through her hair and framing her face as he brought her mouth back to his. "That wedding today started me thinking. I probably shouldn't be saying this, but…" His voice trailed off as he began to undress her.

She shivered in anticipation as she helped him strip the maid of honor dress off her heated body.

"But?" she pressed, doing her best to urge him on.

He began to kiss her face, talking in between the kisses they were sharing.

"But for the first time in my life, it made me wonder what it might be like being part of a duo, a couple. A married couple," he emphasized, feeling as if he was tripping over his own tongue again.

Chris was raining kisses over her face, making himself increasingly more excited with every moment that passed.

"I'm sure you had plenty of opportunity to find out," she told him, breathing heavily as each kiss blossomed into something that seemed more and more overwhelming to her.

"Not really," he told her honestly. "I wasn't one of those guys who had time to play around. There was always something to be done that got in the way." He paused, kissing her soundly and with feeling. "Roe?"

Her heart was pounding so hard, she could hardly hear him. "Yes?" she asked hoarsely.

"Do you really want to talk?"

Rather than answer his question, she raised her head, took his face between her hands and pressed her lips against his, silently giving him his answer.

All conversation was tabled for approximately the next ninety minutes until they both fell back onto her bed, completely and utterly exhausted and spent.

The room was filled with nothing but the sound of their heavy breathing.

And then, finally, he was able to say her name one more time, barely above a whisper. "Roe?"

With delicious sensations throbbing through her body, she turned her head in his direction. "Is this going to be another trick question?" she asked Chris in a low whisper.

"I hope not," he told her. Gathering his courage, he turned his body completely toward hers and asked, his voice barely audible, "How do you feel about getting married?"

For a moment, he had caught her completely off guard and she was stunned.

"Is this a quiz, or an actual serious question?" she finally asked.

"A serious question," he answered.

She still felt he couldn't be asking her what it appeared he was asking. It seemed to her that she had been waiting to hear this question from him for what felt like most of her life, ever since she had first set eyes on him.

Still, she proceeded cautiously. "Married to whom?" she asked.

He waved his hand at her. She was being evasive, which he felt was her way of avoiding giving an answer. "Never mind."

Roe propped herself up on her elbow, fixing him with a penetrating look. "Maybe I just want to hear the words and be asked. Did you ever think of that?"

"All right." This was a lot harder than he had initially thought. Bracing himself, he asked, "Would you consider marrying me?"

"I would, if you could word it a little more romantically than how you would place a take-out order," she told him.

He paused for a moment, as if stumped and debating just how to properly word his question, then he asked, "Rosemary Robertson, would you make me one of the happiest men on the face of the earth by saying that you would marry me?"

Roe moved her body closer to his, her expression glowing. He had said the words she had fantasized about hearing all those many years ago.

"Yes," she whispered. "Yes, I would!" she declared far more loudly.

Chris hadn't thought he had an ounce of strength left within him, but it seemed to have risen up from somewhere as he drew her back into his arms, suddenly wanting her with a fierceness he was entirely unfamiliar with.

"Then come tomorrow morning, I'm going to ask

your grandfather for your hand in marriage—as well as for the rest of you, too," he teased, kissing her again.

"You're sure?" she questioned, her eyes searching his face for some indication that he actually meant what he was saying.

"I've never been more sure of anything in my whole life, Roe," he told her.

But she still couldn't get herself to believe he actually meant it. "You're not just getting carried away with the wedding and other things?"

"I don't get carried away," he reminded her. "Except maybe by the taste of your lips," he told her as he brought his mouth to hers again.

She put her hands up against his chest, creating a wedge between them. She wanted him to be completely sure. "You can change your mind, you know. In case you realize that you've just gotten carried away, you are allowed to change your mind," she told him seriously.

He raised his head, searching her face. "Are you trying to talk me out of it?"

"Oh heavens no, never that," she told him in all seriousness just before she kissed him again.

This time, he believed her.

When they told Roe's grandfather several days later, having waited so that they didn't take anything away from Riley's celebration, he, as well as her mother and sisters, were all beside themselves with the joy of anticipating yet another wedding.

The last one.

After giving his permission and then hugging his only single granddaughter, Mike turned toward Rita. "All I can say is that thank goodness you didn't have quintuplets, Rita. I don't think that my heart could take two more weddings after this one," the older man said, laughing.

"When can I get married, Pop?" Vikki asked, gleefully looking at everyone in the room and planning her own ceremony.

"You?" Mike questioned as he turned to look at the little girl. "I thought you said you didn't want to get married."

Vikki raised her chin defiantly. "I changed my mind, Pop," she informed the only grandfather she had ever known. "Getting married looks like a lot of fun now."

"It might be," Matt told his daughter with a nod, "but not for a long, long time."

"But you had fun," Vikki said, pouting as she looked from her father to her stepmother. Her expression was accusatory.

"And when you're older, so will you," Matt promised. "But not yet and not now. Okay?" he asked, his eyes meeting Vikki's.

The little redhead sighed dramatically. "Okay," she reluctantly agreed. "But I get to be Aunt Roe's flower girl," she said, bargaining with her father and her stepmother. Her eyes shifted from one to the other like little tennis balls. "Is that a deal?"

Her parents, Matt and Riley, exchanged looks with one another as well as with the newest couple-to-be. It was hard to say who was more amused. "Deal!" everyone proclaimed almost in unison.

No one was happier about this state of affairs than Mike and his daughter-in-law, Rita.

Except, of course, the newest married-couple-to-be.

Epilogue

Roe smiled at her reflection in the mirror. Her wedding was now three and a half months behind her, and it still brought a smile to her lips whenever she thought of it and relived entire segments.

Of course, she had attended her sisters' ceremonies, but the memory of her own wedding brought the biggest sentimental smile to her lips.

Maybe she was being prejudice, but hers still felt as if it had been the most special ceremony of all.

Or maybe she felt that way because of something else, she thought with a wide smile.

Turning sideways, Roe looked herself over in the mirror, wondering how long it would be before she would actually start to show.

It was still hard for her to really believe it. Not that

she had wound up marrying the man of her dreams, but that she was actually carrying around a little Christopher or a little Roe within her.

She couldn't wait to tell the others.

Who would have ever thought?

Chris would have, she silently reassured herself. They had hardly been married for more than a day when she caught him looking at her with that odd smile of his. When she had asked him what he was thinking, he'd told her, "Just envisioning that lovely body of yours with our baby growing inside of you."

She had waved him off with a laugh.

Soon after that, Raegan had surprised everyone by making an announcement at Sunday dinner that she was pregnant.

It had taken a bit of explaining what that meant to Vikki, but after a bit, everything swiftly and satisfactorily fell into place for the little girl.

It took more explaining when three weeks later, Riley made the same announcement at another family Sunday dinner. A lot more explaining, as well as a bit of reassuring that the "little stranger" on the way was not about to replace Vikki in her parents' eyes or their affections, as she feared might wind up happening.

"Nobody is *ever* going to take your place, Sweetheart," Riley promised the little girl. "As a matter of fact, we're counting on you to be a big sister and help us take care of this baby," she told her stepdaughter. "Do you think you can do that?" she asked Vikki.

Vikki solemnly bobbed her head up and down. "Uh-huh."

Roe couldn't help wondering now how Vikki was going to take this latest piece of news. Well, she hoped, mentally crossing her fingers.

In a time-honored, eternal gesture, she placed her hand protectively over her abdomen. "Wow, who would have ever thunk it?" she murmured to herself.

Knocking on their bedroom door—they spent their time on the ranch, but kept her place in town for her veterinarian practice—Christopher peeked in.

"Are you about ready to go?" he asked.

"Just about," she answered, smoothing out her skirt.

"Who were you talking to?" he asked her innocently, pretending to look around the room.

She avoided his eyes. "Nobody."

"Oh, I thought maybe it was the baby," he said, coming up behind her.

Roe's eyes met his in the mirror as she looked at him in surprise. "What baby?"

Turning her around, his eyes dipped down to her abdomen. "That one."

Her mouth fell opened as she looked at him, stunned. "How did you—?"

"I was there at the time, remember?" he said, referring to their wedding night. "Besides, I heard you throwing up the other night."

She had tried so hard to hide everything. "I thought you were asleep."

"I know. I wasn't," he told her. "I was just waiting for you to say something," he said just before he swept her into his arms for a heartfelt hug.

"So you're happy?" she asked him innocently.

"What do you think?" Chris laughed. "Boy, are your grandfather and mother going to be overjoyed," he predicted just before he kissed her again.

"You're kidding? You're not kidding, are you?" Mike asked joyfully, looking at Roe and her husband. They had barely begun eating their dinner before Roe, unable to wait any longer, had made her announcement.

"When?" Rita asked about this latest grandchild's due date.

"Approximately five and a half months from now," Roe answered.

Mike looked at Chris. This latest great-grandson-in-law hadn't said a word. "Cat got your tongue, boy?"

"I figured this was her announcement to make," Chris said good-naturedly.

"You realize that nobody is going to believe this," Matt said, looking around the table. "Triplets all pregnant at approximately the same time."

"Doesn't matter what anyone else believes," Alan told the others with a wave of his hand. "It just matters what we all know." He looked around at the people seated at the table and smiled. "Right?"

"Right," Raegan agreed, her hand cupping her own growing stomach.

"What about me?" Vikki asked, looking at the grown-ups seated around her.

"You get to be the big sister. Everyone's big sister," her father told her, trying to reassure the little girl.

Vikki nodded her head solemnly, accepting her new role in all this. "Okay."

She had no idea why everyone laughed at that, but it was a nice, warming sound so she smiled as well.

"Eat, people," Mike urged his granddaughters as well as their husbands. "You're all going to need your strength," he predicted, taking another helping. "Heaven knows I certainly am."

His words were met with more laughter.

Smiling at the younger people, Mike went on eating. He thought back to his conversation with Roe in the stable about the sadness he was experiencing. Contrary to his statement, he thought about what a very lucky man he had turned out to be.

An incredibly warm feeling filled his heart. And went on filling it for a very long time to come.

* * * * *

SPECIAL EXCERPT FROM

Dr. Grace Hollister has her hands full running a busy practice and single-parenting her young son. Veterinarian Mack Barlow is swamped with four-legged patients, running a ranch and being the sole provider to his little daughter.

When these exes meet, old sparks reignite in new ways. This couple is overdue for a second chance at love. But only if Grace can trust Mack with her heart again.

Read on for a sneak preview of
Rancher to the Rescue
by Stella Bagwell.

Chapter One

Grace Hollister was wearily slipping one arm out of her lab coat when a voice called to her from the open doorway of her office.

"I hate to be the messenger to bring you bad news, Doctor, but you have one more patient to see before we shut the doors."

Grace turned a questioning look at Cleo, one of two nurses who assisted her throughout the busy days at Pine Valley Clinic.

"I do? I thought Mr. Daniels was the last one."

Cleo stepped into the small space and Grace shrugged the white garment back onto her shoulder.

"Harper scheduled a last-minute walk-in," the nurse explained. "Guess she was feeling softhearted."

In spite of being bone-tired, Grace managed to

chuckle at Cleo's explanation for the clinic's receptionist. "Harper is always softhearted. And her tongue refuses to form the word *no*."

"In this case, I don't think you would've wanted Harper to turn this patient away. She's five years old and as cute as her father."

Sighing, Grace reached for a stethoscope lying on the corner of her desk and motioned for the petite brunette to precede her out of the office. "Since when have you started eyeing married men?"

The two women started down a short hallway to where three separate examining rooms were located. As they walked, Cleo answered in a hushed voice, "If there's a wife, she's not listed on the patient's information sheet."

Grace rolled her eyes. Being twenty-five and single, Cleo was always looking for Mr. Right. So far, she'd not found him. But it wasn't for lack of trying.

"Hmm. I suppose it was necessary for you to take a peek at the parent-guardian information."

The nurse slanted a guilty glance at Grace. "My eyes just happened to land on that part of the paper."

"You're hopeless, Cleo."

"Yes, but this place would be boring without me."

No, without her two nurses, Cleo and Poppy, the flow of patients going in and out of the clinic would be reduced to a crawl, Grace thought.

"Like watching grass grow," Grace joked, then quickly switched to serious mode. "Is the child in room two?"

That particular examining room was referred to by Grace and the staff as the kid-friendly room. The walls were adorned with playful paintings of animals and clowns, while colorful balloons floated from the handles on the cabinets.

"Yes. And her dad is with her." Cleo followed Grace to the next closed door. "If you can handle this patient without me, I'll help Poppy finish tidying up three."

Grace pulled a clipboard from a holder on the wall and began to scan the patient's information. "I'll call—"

Her words broke off abruptly as she stared in disbelief at the signature at the bottom of the paper. The cursive writing was barely legible, yet the name seemed to leap off the page.

Mackenzie Barlow!

"Doc, is anything wrong? You look sick!"

Tearing her gaze off the signature, Grace glanced over at Cleo. The nurse was studying her closely.

"Uh...no. Nothing is wrong." Even though she was trying her best to sound normal, she could hear a tremble in her voice. "I'm tired, that's all. Go help Poppy. If I need you I'll find you."

Cleo cast her a skeptical look before she walked on down the hallway and entered room three. Once the nurse was out of sight, Grace drew in a bracing breath and passed a hand over her forehead.

You're a physician, Grace. A professional. It doesn't matter that you once planned to marry Mack.

You've been taught to turn off your emotions. So turn them off and go do your job.

Determined to follow the goading voice going off in her head, Grace straightened her shoulders. Then, after giving the door a cursory knock, she stepped into the room to find a small, dark-haired girl sitting on the edge of the examining table.

Purposely keeping her focus on the patient, Grace smiled at the girl, who was dressed in a fuzzy red sweater and blue jeans that were stuffed into a pair of sparkly pink cowboy boots. A single braid rested on one shoulder, while her arms were hugging protectively against her midsection. The heels of her boots were thumping rhythmically against the vinyl padding on the end of the table.

To her immediate right, Grace sensed Mack rising from a plastic waiting chair, but she didn't acknowledge his presence. Instead, she closed the short distance between her and the patient and introduced herself.

"Hello, young lady." She held her hand out to the girl. "I'm Dr. Grace. And I believe your name is Kitty. Is that right?"

The girl hesitated for only a moment and then with an affirmative nod, she placed her hand in Grace's. "I'm Kitty Barlow. And I'm five years old."

Grace gave the child a reassuring smile. "Five. I'm going to guess you're in kindergarten."

Kitty nodded again, but she didn't look a bit proud of the fact.

A couple of steps behind her, Mack said, "Hello, Grace."

Slowly, she turned and faced the man who'd once held her heart in his hand. As her gaze settled on his face, everything around them turned into a dim haze. "Hello, Mack. How are you?"

Over the years Grace had often imagined how she might react if she ever saw Mackenzie again. But none of those scenarios came close to matching this moment. Pain, joy and longing were flashing through her as though their parting had only happened yesterday.

He offered her his hand, and as she reached to wrap her fingers around his, she hoped he couldn't detect the cataclysmic effect he was having on her.

"Fine, thanks," he replied. "And I want to apologize for showing up at such a late hour. I imagine you normally shut the doors before now."

Her throat was so tight she was surprised her vocal cords could form a sound. "Normally. But not always."

Fourteen years. That's how much time had passed since Grace had seen this man. The long years had changed him, she realized, but only for the better. The nineteen-year-old she'd been so in love with had evolved into a rugged hunk of man with broad shoulders, a lean waist and long sinewy legs. Beneath a battered gray cowboy hat, his dark hair was now long enough to curl over the back of his collar. Yet it was his face that had appeared to change the most, she thought. The youthful features she remembered were now hardened lines and angles carved from a weathered, dark brown skin that matched his deep-set eyes.

He said, “I appreciate you taking the time to see Kitty. My schedule has been pretty hectic here lately. But I'm sure you're accustomed to hectic schedules.”

“Doctors are busy people,” she said, then cleared her throat, withdrew her hand from his and turned back to his daughter.

“Well now, Kitty, I'd like to hear how you've been feeling. This paper on my clipboard says you've been having tummy aches. Can you tell me how your tummy feels when you get sick?”

Kitty's big brown eyes made an uneasy sweep of Grace's face before she finally nodded. “It hurts a lot—like it squeezes together.”

Grace fitted the stethoscope to her ears. “Well, I'm going to do my best to make all the squeezing go away,” she said gently. “Can you tell me when your tummy hurts? Before or after you eat? When you go to bed or go to school?”

“In the mornings—when I get ready for school. And it hurts at school. I want to put my head on the desk, but teacher says if I feel bad I need to go home. So Daddy comes and gets me.”

Grace turned a questioning look at Mack and she didn't miss the lines of worry on his face.

He said, “I've had to pick her up at school a couple of times in the past two weeks and then again today.”

“I see.” She turned back to the child. “Okay, Kitty,

I want you to lie back on the table for me. I'm going to figure out what's causing these tummy aches."

For the next few minutes Grace gave the girl a slow, methodical examination. Throughout the inspection of Kitty's physical condition, Mack remained standing, but thankfully he didn't interrupt Grace with questions. Even so, with his watchful presence, it was a fight for Grace to remain focused on her job.

"Do you think her appendix needs to come out?" Mack asked. "Or does she have a hernia? I know kids her age can get them and she's always climbing and jumping."

"I don't believe we're dealing with anything along those lines," she told him as she gathered up her clipboard. "Wait here. We'll talk in a minute."

Grace left the room and headed down the hallway in search of Cleo. She found the nurse in the storage room, restocking a cabinet with paper gowns.

"Cleo, I want you to keep our little patient occupied while I talk with her father in my office. I'll try to make the consultation as quick as possible. I realize everyone is waiting to go home for the night."

Cleo joined her in the open doorway. "Quit worrying about your staff staying late. We know the score around here. Are you feeling better?"

The nurse's question caused Grace's eyes to widen. "Better? There wasn't anything wrong with me."

Cleo shook her head. "You could've fooled me."

Grace did her best not to smirk. “Send Mack… uh, Mr. Barlow to my office.”

The nurse’s eyebrows arched, but she didn’t say anything as she took off in long strides toward the examining room.

In her office, Grace took a seat behind a large desk and resisted the urge to run a hand over her hair, or look to see if any of the lipstick she’d applied earlier in the day was still on her lips. How she looked to Mack Barlow hardly mattered. He’d been out of her life for years now. And, anyway, he wasn’t here to see her. This was all about his little daughter.

She barely had time to draw in a deep breath, when a knock sounded on the door.

“Come in,” she called.

Poppy ushered Mack into the room, then closed the door behind her. Grace forced a smile on her face and gestured for him to take a seat in one of the padded armchairs in front of her desk.

“Please make yourself comfortable, Mack.”

He lifted the cowboy hat from his head, then ran a hand over the dark waves before he eased his long, lanky frame into one of the chairs. As he settled back into the seat, she noticed for the first time this evening that his clothing was splotched with dust and manure. Apparently he’d come straight here from the feedlot.

“I’m sure you’re wanting to kick me in the shins right about now,” he said.

Surely he didn’t think she was harboring a grudge

about their breakup all those years ago, she thought. Yes, he had stomped on her heart, but she'd survived and moved on. Besides, her parents had always taught her, and her seven siblings, that carrying a grudge wasn't just harmful, it was sinful.

"Oh. Why? For yanking my ponytail in chemistry class?" she asked impishly. "Don't worry. I've forgiven you."

Grinning faintly, he raked a hand over his hair for a second time and Grace couldn't help but notice how a thick dark wave fell onto the right side of his forehead.

"Actually, I was referring to a few minutes ago," he said. "I shouldn't have asked you to explain Kitty's health in front of her. I know better than that—but I've been worried about her. I, uh… It's not always easy trying to be both mother and father. Especially now that I have so many things going on with the ranch and my vet practice. I…don't get to spend as much time with her as I should."

So there wasn't a mother in the picture, Grace thought. What could've have happened? A divorce? His wife died? She could pose the question as a medical one. Kitty's lack of a mother could possibly be affecting her health. But given their past history, Grace doubted Mack would view the question as a professional one.

Instead, she said, "I heard about your father's death. Will was a special man. Everyone in the area thought highly of him."

"Thanks. Losing him—it's still a shock. I have to keep reminding myself that he's really gone. Especially now that I'm living on the Broken B. I expect to look around the house and see him. Or find him down at the barns, or spot him riding across the range."

About two months ago, Mack's father had died unexpectedly from a sudden heart attack. Grace hadn't gone to the funeral. At the time, her appointment book had been crammed full and she'd mentally argued that trying to reschedule patients would've been a nightmare for Harper. Plus, closing the clinic for the day, for any reason, always caused double loads of work for the staff later on. Yet in all honesty, Grace had skipped saying a public farewell to Will because she couldn't summon the courage to face Mack. And she'd regretted it ever since.

"I'm sorry I wasn't at the funeral. But I—"

He interrupted her with a shake of his head. "No need to explain. I'm sure you were busy. And, anyway, your parents and brothers were there. That meant a lot to me."

Grace felt like a bug crawling across the hardwood floor of her office. "My family always thought highly of your parents. As did I."

He gave her a single nod. "I've not forgotten."

No, Grace thought. There'd been too much between them to forget completely. She cleared her throat, then steered the conversation back to his daughter.

"Well, regarding Kitty, it's perfectly natural for

you to be concerned and ask questions. But in your daughter's case, I think you need to quit worrying. She's going to be fine…in time."

His dark eyebrows arched upward. "In time? What does that mean?"

Grace was amazed that she could sit here talking to him in a normal voice, while inside she felt as if a tornado was tearing a path from her head to her feet.

"First off, let me say I'm not detecting anything seriously wrong with Kitty's stomach. There's no bloating, bulges, lumps or bumps or sensitive spots that I could detect, and her digestive sounds are normal. She told me she doesn't throw up. Is that true?"

"No. Her meals stay down. She just holds a hand to her stomach and says it hurts."

Grace thoughtfully tapped the end of a pen against a notepad lying on the desktop. "Hmm. When did these stomachaches start?"

"About two weeks ago—after she started school."

Grace nodded. "Does your daughter like school?"

"When we lived in Nevada, she loved nursery school and all her friends. She adored her teacher. But now that we moved up here everything is different for her. She says the other kids look at her funny and the teacher is always telling her to be quiet. Which is understandable. At times, Kitty can be a chatterbox." Frowning, he leaned forward in his seat. "Do you think my daughter is pretending to be sick so she won't have to go to school?"

"No. I believe she's honestly experiencing stomach pains and I have a notion they're all stemming from the stress of moving to a strange place and leaving her friends behind. Tell me, has Kitty lived in multiple places or is this the first move for her?"

He shook his head. "Ever since she was born, we've lived on the KO Ranch, not far from Reno. That's the only home she's ever known. I was a resident vet there."

Grace couldn't contain her interest. "Oh. Must've been a huge ranch. Stone Creek can't afford a resident vet. Although, Dad often wishes he could."

He shrugged. "It was a good place to live and work. And a nice place to raise Kitty. But with Dad's death…well, I want to keep the Broken B going. And I'm hoping the ranch will come to be a good home for her."

She nodded. "I've not forgotten how hard your parents worked to make the Broken B profitable. I'm sure the ranch is very important to you."

He cleared his throat and glanced to the wall on his right, where a wide window was shuttered with woven blinds. "Mom and Dad wanted that place for me. I guess—" His gaze settled back on her face. "Now that I have Kitty I understand what it actually means to build a legacy."

More than once in their young romance, they'd talked about the children they would have and their plans to build their own ranch, together. Unfortunately, some dreams were meant to die, she thought sadly.

The stinging at the back of her eyes caused her to blink several times before she could focus clearly on the prescription pad lying on the desktop.

"Well, uh, I think the issue with Kitty's stomach will take a little time. Once she gets more settled she should begin to feel better. In the meantime, I'm going to prescribe something mild to soothe her tummy. And don't worry, it's nothing she can become dependent on."

"So how long does she need to take this medication? And if she doesn't get better soon, how long should I wait to bring her back to see you?"

"Give her two more weeks, at least. And then if you don't see an improvement, bring her back to see me and we'll take things from there. Right now, I'd rather not put her through a bunch of unnecessary testing. It would only put more stress on her."

"Yes, I agree."

"Do you want a paper prescription? Or I can call your pharmacy?"

"You still do the paper thing?"

Even though her nerves were rapidly breaking down, his question put a smile on her face. "I do. Some of my elderly patients feel more at ease when they have a piece of paper in their hand. And anything I can do to make them feel better is my job. I'm sure you feel that way about your patients, too."

He smiled back at her and she thought how different it was from the carefree grins he gave her all those years ago. Now she could see the everyday strains of life etched beneath his eyes and around his lips.

"Only my patients can't talk to me. At least, not in words. A kick, or bite or scratch pretty much tells me what they're thinking about Dr. Barlow."

She chuckled. "Sometimes I wish my patients couldn't talk."

She reached for the prescription pad and hurriedly scratched out the necessary information. Once she was finished, she stood and rounded the desk. At the same time, Mack rose from the chair.

She handed him the small square of paper. "Here's the prescription. If you have any questions about the dosage, just call the office," she told him. "Now, I'll go say goodbye to Kitty and the two of you will be ready to go."

"Thank you, Grace. I, uh, already feel better about Kitty."

She gave him an encouraging smile. "Have faith. Time heals."

He shot her an odd look and then a stoic expression shuttered his face. "I'll keep that in mind."

As Grace followed him out of the office, she realized her remark had struck some sort of chord with him. Perhaps she should have made it clear that she was referring to Kitty's problem, she thought. He'd lost so much in his life already. His mother and father. And somehow, he'd lost Kitty's mother, too. Maybe he'd considered Grace's comment as being trite or even insulting.

Why should it matter if you've bruised Mack's feelings? Toughen up, Grace. It hadn't bothered him to stomp all over your hopes and dreams.

As the two of them walked down the hallway to the waiting area at the front of the clinic, Grace tried to push away the nagging voice in her head. And for the most part, she succeeded. However, she didn't have any luck at ignoring Mack's tall presence.

The way he walked, the lanky way he moved and the scent of the outdoors drifting from his clothes all reminded her of how much she'd once loved having his arms crushing her close to him, his lips devouring hers.

Oh, Lord, how could those memories still be so vivid in her mind? she wondered. She'd just told Mack that time heals. And yet time had done little to wipe him from her memory bank.

When they reached the waiting room, Cleo was reading a story to Kitty from a children's book, but as soon as the child spotted her father, the story was forgotten. She jumped from the short couch and ran straight to his side.

Grabbing a tight hold on his hand, she asked, "Can we go home now, Daddy?"

"Yes, we're going home. As soon as you thank Dr. Grace for taking care of you."

Grace squatted to put herself on the child's level and as she studied Kitty's sweet face, she could see so very much of Mack in her features. She had his rich brown eyes and dark hair. And her little square chin and the dimple carving her left cheek was a miniature replica of her father's.

"It was nice meeting you, Kitty. And I hope your tummy gets better really soon. I'm giving your daddy some medicine to give you so you won't hurt. Will you take it for me?"

Kitty wrinkled her nose as she contemplated Grace's question. "Does it taste awful?"

Numerous children passed through the clinic on a weekly basis and they all touched Grace's heart in one way or another. But none of them had pulled on her heartstrings the way Kitty was yanking on hers at this very moment.

Smiling, Grace said, "Not at all. It tastes like cherries."

"Oh, I guess it will be okay then."

"That's a good girl. And there's something else I'd like for you to do."

Kitty's eyes narrowed skeptically. "What? Take a shot?"

Grace glanced up to see a look of amusement on Mack's face, and without thinking, she gave him a conspiring wink. He winked back and suddenly the tense knots inside Grace begin to ease.

Turning her attention back to Kitty, she said, "No. You don't need a shot. I want you to promise me that when you go to school tomorrow you won't be afraid that your tummy is going to hurt. And you'll try your best to make friends with your classmates."

As soon as Grace spoke the word *friends*, Kitty's

lips pursed into a pout. "But the other kids don't like me," she said with a shake of her head.

"Do they really tell you that they don't like you? Or do you just have a feeling that they don't?"

Kitty glanced up at her father as though she wanted him to rescue her. When he didn't, her chin dropped against her chest. "No. They don't tell me that," she mumbled. "But they won't talk to me—that's how I know."

Grace patted the girl's little shoulder. "Maybe they're waiting on you to talk to them first. Why don't you try it tomorrow? I'll bet you'll find out they'd like to talk to you. Do you have a horse or a dog?"

Her head shot up and she nodded eagerly. "I have both! My horse is Moonpie and my dog is Rusty."

"That's nice. So you can talk to them about Moonpie and Rusty and tell them all the things you and your pets do on the ranch. Do you think you can do that?"

To Grace's relief, Kitty gave her a huge nod.

"Good girl!"

After giving Kitty another encouraging pat, she straightened to her full height and turned to Mack.

"Thank you, Grace."

His gaze was roaming over her face as though he was trying to read her thoughts. The idea caused a ball of emotion to suddenly form in her throat.

"You're welcome," she said, barely managing to get out the words. "And if Kitty has any more problems, let me know."

"I will," he assured her.

Father and daughter started toward the door and as Grace watched them go, she was struck by a sense of loss.

"Goodbye, Kitty."

The girl turned and gave Grace a little wave. "Bye, Dr. Grace. Thank you."

Once the pair had stepped outside and the door closed behind them, Cleo immediately jumped to her feet.

"You knew that man! Why didn't you tell me?"

Grace felt her cheeks growing warm. Which was a ridiculous reaction. She shouldn't feel awkward about being acquainted with Mack.

"I hardly thought it mattered," Grace said.

"Grace! He's hot! Hot! Of course, it matters!"

"To you, maybe. Not to me."

Turning away from the nurse, Grace walked over to a low counter separating the waiting area from Harper's reception desk. The young woman with short, platinum-blond hair was busy typing information into a computer, but glanced up as soon as she noticed Grace's presence.

"Shut everything down, Harper," Grace told her. "I'm sorry you stayed so late. You should've gone home before this last patient."

The young woman shook her head. "No problem, Doctor. I thought I'd stay, just in case you needed to schedule the girl another appointment."

"Thanks for being so thoughtful, Harper, but that won't be necessary. At least, not for now."

A few steps behind her, Cleo let out a wistful sigh. "Grace, I don't understand why you didn't suggest a follow-up. You could have included the cost with this visit."

Rolling her eyes toward the ceiling, Grace turned to the nurse. "Cleo, if you weren't so indispensable, I'd fire you."

Cleo giggled. "Oh, come on! I can't help it. It's not every day we get to see a guy like Mr. Barlow. So where did you know him from?"

Not wanting to overreact and cause the nurse to be suspicious, she answered in the most casual voice she could summon. "He's an old classmate. That's all."

"Oh. I thought—"

"What?"

Grace's one-word question must've sounded sharp because Cleo suddenly looked a bit shamefaced.

"Uh…nothing. If you don't need anything else, I'll go tell Poppy we're closing up."

"I'd appreciate that, Cleo. It's been a long day," Grace told her. "And right now I just want to pick up Ross and go home."

She started down the hallway to her office and Cleo walked briskly at her side.

"Grace, I'm sorry if talking about Mr. Barlow offended you. I never thought it would make you… well, angry with me."

Holding back a sigh, Grace said, "Forget it, Cleo. I'm not angry. And if I sounded cranky, just chalk it up to exhaustion."

"Is Kitty going to be okay, you think?"

"Yes. In time."

"That's good. She's an adorable little girl. Too bad she doesn't have a mother," Cleo said,

"How do you know she doesn't have a mother?"

"Because she told me so. While I was sitting with her in the waiting room."

Pausing in midstride, Grace shot the sassy nurse a look of disbelief. "Oh, Cleo, don't tell me you pumped the child for personal information!"

"No! I promise, Grace, I didn't. She asked me if I had any kids and I told her no. That's when she told me she'd never had a mommy."

Never had a mommy. Grace could only wonder what that possibly meant.

"I see. Well, you know how children are. They say things in different ways. Hopefully she has one somewhere. Because right now she could certainly use one."

Before Cleo could reply, Poppy stepped out of a nearby storage room. As she joined them in the middle of the hallway, she glanced pointedly at her watch. "Should I go ahead and call the Wagon Spoke for four orders of eggs and toast? Someone at the café might take pity on us and deliver it here to the clinic."

Grace released a good-natured groan. "I'm definitely starving. But, no. Let's turn off the lights and get out of here."

Twenty minutes later, Grace picked up her seven-year-old son, Ross, at the babysitter's house, which fortunately was located only two doors down from her own home.

Ross was accustomed to his mother's erratic work hours, but this evening as she unlocked the front door, he was complaining. Grace could hardly blame him. Tonight she was an hour and a half behind schedule.

"Gosh, Mom, I didn't think you were ever going show up! I'm starving!"

"Didn't Birdie make dinner for the twins?"

Besides babysitting Ross after school on weekdays, Birdie held down a computer job that allowed her to work from home. Divorced and in her early thirties, she had twin boys two years older than Ross. Normally, if Grace was working late, Birdie would have Ross eat dinner with them.

"Birdie had a lot of extra work to do. So she's just now cooking dinner," Ross explained. "She gave us cookies and milk when we got home from school, but I'm starving now."

With a hand on his shoulder, Grace guided her son into the house. As they passed through the living room, Ross tossed his schoolbooks into an armchair and Grace placed her purse and briefcase on a wall table.

"I've had a long list of patients today, honey," Grace explained as she tiredly raked a loose strand of blond hair away from her face. "That's why I'm late."

Ross paused to look at her, and as Grace took in his slim face, blue eyes and wavy blond hair falling across his forehead, Mack's words came back to her.

Now that I have Kitty I understand what it actually means to build a legacy.

Yes, Grace understood, too. She was Ross's sole parent. It was her responsibility and deepest concern to provide her son with a good home and a solid future.

It's not always easy being a mother and father to Kitty.

No, Grace thought, sometimes it was achingly hard to be a single parent. She could've told Mack she knew all about being both father and mother, but she'd kept the personal information to herself. He hadn't brought Kitty to the clinic in order to learn about Grace's private life. In fact, she doubted he cared one whit about her marital status.

"Mom, why are you looking at me so funny?"

Ross's question interrupted her thoughts and she let out a weary breath and patted him on top of the head.

"Sorry, Ross. I was just being a mommy and thinking how much I love you."

He groaned and scuffed the toe of his athletic shoe against the hardwood floor. "Aww, Mom. That's mushy stuff. Boys don't want to hear mushy stuff."

Chuckling now, she playfully scrubbed the top of his head, then shooed him out of the room. "Okay. No more mushy stuff. Go change and wash and I'll see what I can find in the kitchen."

Ross started down the hallway to where the bedrooms were located, then stopped midway to look back at his mother.

"Can we have pizza?" he asked eagerly. "Just for tonight?"

Being a doctor, Grace had tried to instill good eating habits in her son. But that didn't mean she was a strict prude and never allowed him, or herself, to eat something simply because it tasted good.

"Sure we can. As long as you eat some salad with it."

"Okay! Thanks, Mom!"

He raced on down the hallway and as Grace headed to the kitchen, her thoughts unwittingly drifted to Mack and Kitty. The drive from town to the Broken B consisted of more than fifteen miles of rough dirt road. And once they arrived at the big old ranch house, it would be empty. Just like this one.

Maybe he preferred living a solitary life, she thought. But Grace couldn't help but wonder if he might think of her as he went about his nightly chores. Moreover, had she ever crossed his mind since that awful day fourteen years ago when he'd told her their romance was over? Had he ever felt a twinge of regret?

No. Mack wasn't the sort to have regrets, she thought. She remembered him as being the type of guy who, once he made a decision, plowed forward and never looked back. And that was the same way she needed to deal with her own life. Plow forward and forget she ever knew Mack Barlow.

Chapter Two

"Daddy, why don't I have a mommy to braid my hair?"

In Kitty's bedroom, Mack stood behind his daughter, who was sitting on a padded bench in front of the dresser. Braiding her long, dark hair was something he'd done since she was a toddler and the chore came as natural to him as bridling a horse.

"Because you have a daddy to do it for you instead of a mommy," he told her.

From the corner of his eye, he could see her image in the dresser mirror, and the frown on her face said she was far from satisfied with his answer. The fact hardly surprised Mack. The older that Kitty got, the more questions she had. Especially questions concerning her mother.

"But why don't I have a mommy? The kids at school have one."

"All of them?"

"Yes! Every one of them!"

He made a tsking noise with his tongue. "Kitty. I've told you to always tell the truth. Are you telling me the truth now?"

She huffed out a heavy breath. "Oh, Daddy— Okay. I don't know for sure if they *all* have mommies. They say they do."

He fastened the end of the braid with a red scrunchie, then gave her shoulders a pat. "Well, you don't have one because she—"

When he paused, Kitty twisted around on the dressing bench and looked up at him. "'Cause why? 'Cause she don't love me?"

Oh, God, I'm not equipped for this, Mack thought. And he especially didn't need this sort of father-daughter talk this morning. If they didn't leave the house in fifteen minutes, she was going to be late getting to school and Mack's veterinary clinic would be overrun with patients before he ever got there.

With his hands on her shoulders, Mack gently turned his daughter around to face him. "Don't ever think such a thing, Kitty. She loved you and that's why she gave you to me—so I could take good care of you."

Frowning with confusion, Kitty's head tilted to one side. "Why couldn't she take care of me?"

From the moment Kitty had begun to talk and

form whole sentences, Mack had learned that one question always led to another. Most of the time his daughter's quest for answers was amusing. But not this morning. Talking about Kitty's mother was like prying the scab off a wound. Not that he regretted having a child with the woman. No. He wouldn't trade Kitty for anything in his life. He only wished, for Kitty's sake, that their relationship had been something more than a meaningless affair.

"Well, because your mommy was different. She was like a bird. To be happy, birds have to fly free—to far-off places."

"But she can't be a bird, Daddy. She can't fly."

Mack bit back a sigh, while at the same time admiring his daughter's ability to see the reality of the situation.

Mack said, "No. She doesn't have wings or anything like that. I only meant that she has to keep traveling. But I promise that she thinks about you."

To his relief a smile spread across her face. "Really?"

"Yes. Really." He patted her cheek. "Now go find your boots and get your red coat. It's going to be colder today."

She jumped off the dressing bench. "Can I wear my red cowboy boots, too? The ones with the stars on the tops?"

"Sure. But don't drag your toes on the concrete."

"Okay." She started toward the closet, then halfway there, turned to look at him. "Daddy?"

"Yes."

"Will I get to see Dr. Grace again?"

The question caught him off guard. Last night after they'd left the clinic, she'd talked briefly about the examination Grace had given her, but after that, she'd not mentioned Grace or anything about the doctor's visit. Mack had assumed his daughter had already dismissed the whole experience.

"I don't think so. Unless you get sick again. And you don't want that to happen, do you?"

"No! I'm going to do like Dr. Grace told me. I'm not gonna think about my tummy!" Momentarily forgetting her father's order to fetch her boots and coat, she took a few steps toward him. "She was really nice and pretty. Did you think so?"

Unfortunately, he'd been thinking those very things and a whole lot more he shouldn't have been thinking. "She's a nice doctor," he said.

Kitty nodded emphatically. "And she smelled extra good, too! I wish I could smell like her."

Oh, yes, Mack had noticed the soft, sultry scent floating around Grace. He'd also noticed how her silky blond hair brushed the tops of her shoulders and the way her black slacks and sweater had clung to her feminine curves. The passing years had been sweet to her, he thought. Even under the harsh fluorescent lighting, her ivory skin had appeared flawless, her blue eyes bright and her pink lips just as full and luscious.

Damn it, he had to be a glutton for punishment,

Mack thought. Instead of taking Kitty to one of the other physicians in town, he'd taken her to a doctor he'd been in love with for all of his adult life.

That thought brought him up short. He wasn't still in love with Grace! That part of his life had ended years ago. Now, she was nothing more than a book of bittersweet memories. One that he hadn't cared to open for a long, long while.

He said, "When you get older I'm fairly certain you'll smell as good as Dr. Grace."

Kitty's smile grew wider. "And be smart like her, too."

"Don't worry, Kitty, you're going to be as smart as you need to be. That is, if you get to school on time." He gestured to the closet, where a pile of clothes spilled out of the small enclosure and onto the bedroom floor. "Now, hurry. Get your boots and coat. I'll wait for you in the kitchen."

Thirty minutes later, Mack dropped off his daughter at Canyon Academy, a private elementary school located in the heart of the small town of Beaver. Then he drove to the western edge of the community where for the past six weeks, carpenters, electricians and plumbers had been working nearly nonstop to transform the old feed and grain store into Barlow Animal Hospital.

Before Mack had purchased the vacated property, the large building with lapboard siding had sported peeling, barn-red paint and a rusty tin roof. Now the siding was a soft gray color and the roof was white metal. Corrals and loafing sheds had been erected at the back of the structure to house large animals, while the interior of the building had been partitioned into smaller rooms, consisting of a treatment area with an adjoining recovery room, two kennel rooms and a break room. At the front entrance of the clinic, there was a large waiting area with a tiled floor and plastic chairs, along with a reception counter.

Mack parked his pickup truck at a gravel parking area at the side of the building, then quickly strode toward a private entryway located at the back.

He was stepping beneath the overhang that sheltered the door, when a tall, sandy-haired cowboy with an anxious look on his face hurried to intercept him.

"Man, am I ever glad to see you!" Oren exclaimed. "There's already a row of vehicles parked out front. Two of them have stock trailers with about eight head of cattle in each one. If we try to do first come, first serve, we'll probably have a riot on our hands."

Three weeks ago, Mack had hired Oren Stratford as his one and only assistant. The young man, who was in his mid-twenties, lived in the nearby town of Minersville and had been working for a well-established veterinarian in Cedar City. Because he'd been looking for a chance to shorten his commute, he'd answered Mack's ad for an assistant. Knowledgeable and friendly, Mack had already developed a good bond with him. But they needed more help in the worst kind of way.

The number of patients passing through the animal clinic each day was growing at a rapid pace and Mack had yet to hire anyone to fill the job of receptionist. So far Mack and Oren were trying to deal with answering the phone and scheduling appointments, along with treating animals.

"We're going to deal with one thing at a time," Mack told him. "The most critical comes first and then on down the line." He opened the door and headed into a narrow hallway with Oren walking alongside him. "Have any idea who arrived first?"

Oren spoke as he followed Mack into the space he'd designated for his office. "Actually, I can tell you that much. A lady with a cat. He has a cyst on his back and at first glance it looks like it's going to need to be cleaned surgically."

Mack switched on a row of overhead fluorescent lights, then flicked on the computer on his desk. "Okay. We'll begin with the cat. Sedate and prep him. Have you turned up the thermostat to the rest of the building?"

"Yes. It's already warm. And I've let the customers into the waiting area. I've taken down names, but that's as far as I gotten with the paperwork."

Mack let out a long breath. "Thanks, Oren. I'd be in a heck of a mess without you. Kitty was dawdling this morning or I would've been here sooner.

Once you have kids, you're going to understand what that means."

Oren chuckled. "I get it, Mack. Mom said as a kid I was the world's worst at dawdling."

"Thank God you grew out of it," Mack said with an amused grin, then quickly shifted gears. "What about the cattle? What's the reason for their visit to the vet?"

"Two separate owners. Vaccinations for one bunch."

Mack groaned. "Doesn't anyone work their own cattle anymore?"

"It's an old man who walks with a cane. Said he couldn't find anybody to come out to his place and help him do the job."

"That's not surprising," Mack said with a grimace. "And the other trailer load?"

"Cow-calf pairs. Looks to me like they might have shipping fever. The guy hasn't had them long. Said he bought them over in Sevier County. But you're the doctor, Mack—you might have a different diagnosis."

"Lord, help us. If that's the case, we'll have to keep them contained and away from the rest of the animals. I'll look them over while you get the cat ready. Anything else?"

"A dog with a torn ear. Doesn't look like it's worth saving to me."

Mack shot him a stunned glance. "The dog?"

"No. The ear. But I could be wrong."

"I hope you're wrong about the ear and the cattle."

The phone began to ring and as Mack reached for the receiver, he jerked a thumb toward the door. "Go on and get the cat ready. I'll deal with this."

More than five hours later, the two men had managed to successfully treat the morning patients and send all of them home except for the cattle with the shipping fever. After they had treated the cow/calf pairs with shots of strong antibiotics and corralled them safely away from the adjoining pens, Mack suggested they take advantage of the time and eat lunch at the Wagon Spoke Café.

Wedged between a saddle shop and an antique shop, the Wagon Spoke had been in business in Beaver for nearly a century. Although, according to the town's history, the eatery moved to its current location after the original building burned down in 1936 from a fire that many old-timers say originated in the kitchen.

Some of Mack's earliest memories were those of his parents bringing him to the café on Saturday nights to eat dinner. Simply furnished, with wooden tables and chairs and one long bar with a green Formica top and matching stools, the place only served ordinary food, but to Mack the outing had always been special for him.

Presently, the front of the old building was sided with a mixture of corrugated iron and asphalt shingles and one large plate glass window overlooking the street. A wide wooden door painted bright green served as the entrance.

As the two men stepped into the busy interior, a cowbell clanged above their heads. To the right, standing behind a long bar, an older waitress with fire-engine-red hair waved to them.

"Seat yourself, boys. Laverne will be with you in a minute."

The two men worked their way through a maze of tables, most of which were occupied with late lunch diners. A couple of men Mack had been acquainted with for years lifted their hands in greeting, while a pair of young women at a nearby table smiled and waved at Oren.

Mack slanted him a sly look. "You obviously have friends here in Beaver."

Oren grinned. "Beaver is only about twenty minutes away from Minersville. And a guy has to do a little socializing. You remember how that is, don't you?"

Mack certainly remembered when he and Grace had been dating. Every minute he'd spent with her had been like a slice of paradise. But after they'd parted, dating or partaking in the social scene had meant little to him.

"I may act old to you, Oren. But I'm not *that* old."

Oren chuckled. "You don't act old, Mack. Just disinterested."

Mack grunted. "Well, Kitty gets what little spare time I have."

The two of them found a vacant table located near the wall at the back of the long room. Once they were seated, Oren looked over at him. “I haven’t had a chance to ask you how Kitty is feeling. You were going to take her to the doctor yesterday evening. How did that go?”

If a man liked having scabs ripped off old sores, Mack supposed the appointment had been successful. But he’d not made the visit to Pine Valley Clinic for himself. It was all for Kitty’s health and nothing else.

Mack said, “It went better than I thought. The doctor prescribed a mild medication and suggested the problem was the stress of being away from her friends and having a new teacher. This morning she seemed to feel perfectly fine and since I’ve not gotten any calls from school yet, I’m keeping my fingers crossed that she’s going to remain that way.”

Oren said, “Moving can be tough on a kid. When I was about ten Dad moved us up to Spanish Fork. My brother and I hated living in town. We were used to roaming outside and being with our best friends. Thank goodness we weren’t there long before we moved back to Minersville.”

“Yeah. Moving to a new place is tough on kids. Tough on adults, too.” Mack shrugged out of his denim jacket and hung it on the back of his chair.

“You almost sound like you regret moving back here to Beaver. What’s wrong? I thought you liked it here,” Oren said.

“Getting into the swing of things here hasn’t been as easy as I’d hoped.” Especially now that he’d come face-to-face with Grace again, he thought ruefully. He'd held the notion that seeing her would be no more than seeing any other old acquaintance. Hell, just how stupid could he get? Just looking at her had been like a hard wham to the side of his head and he still wasn't sure he'd recovered from the blow. "You've heard the old adage you can't go home again? Well, I think that aptly applies to me. I…well, if Dad was still alive it would be different—better."

"If your father was still alive you wouldn't be here, period," Oren reminded him. "You told me you moved back here to take over the Broken B."

"Yeah. That's true. Mom died several years ago, so I'm the only one left now to run the ranch. And for a long time I've been wanting to start my own veterinary business. This move gives me the chance to do both."

Oren opened his mouth to reply when Laverne, a middle-aged waitress with salt-and-pepper hair and a weary smile, walked up to their table and placed plastic-coated menus in front of them.

"You guys look like you could use some coffee," she said.

"Make it hot, Laverne. It's getting colder outside," Oren told her.

"Coming right up."

She left to get the coffee and Mack picked up the menu. A small square of paper with the details of today's special was clipped to the front. As soon as he spotted the words *meat loaf,* he dropped the menu back on the table.

Oren lifted off his cowboy hat, and after placing it in the empty chair next to his, he raked both hands through his hair. "How long has it been since you lived here in Beaver?" he asked.

"About twelve years. Before then, I'd been commuting back and forth from here to college in Cedar City. But after I got my associate degree there, I decided to attend a college in St. George for the rest of my education, so I moved down there. I decided I couldn't do a long commute, attend classes and work a part-time job. I've lived away ever since then. Until Dad died a couple of months ago."

"So you never had the pull to come back here until now?"

Mack supposed most people wouldn't understand his reasoning for staying away. But for a long time he'd associated his hometown with Grace and he'd wanted to forget that idyllic time he'd spent with her. Then later, when his father had told him she'd returned to Beaver from Salt Lake City, he could only think how gut-twisting it would be to see her from afar. At that time he'd never imagined his father would die an early death and send Mack back here to take over his inheritance.

"Kitty and I were just fine down in Nevada," Mack answered. "But we'll be just fine here, too."

Laverne arrived with their coffee and two glasses

of ice water. As she placed the beverages on the table, she looked questioningly at Mack.

"Have you hired anyone to be your receptionist?"

No doubt the waitress probably saw an endless number of people pass through the café on a daily basis and heard just as many stories. Mack was surprised the woman remembered he'd mentioned he'd been on the hunt for someone to fill the job of receptionist for his animal hospital.

"A few persons have inquired about the position. But none were suitable," he told her. "You have someone in mind who'd be good at the job?"

"As a matter of fact, I think I do. I don't know why it didn't cross my mind before now. Eleanor Shipman. She retired from her job about three months ago. Worked twenty years as a receptionist for Denver Garwood over at Independent Insurance. I'd say the woman would know how to answer the phone and schedule things. And I know she's as bored as heck sitting home. No husband or kids to keep her busy, you see."

Mack exchanged hopeful looks with Oren.

"Sounds like she might be the answer," Oren said.

"You have her number?" Mack asked. "I'll give her a call."

"I'll get it when I turn in your orders." She pulled out a pad and pencil. "You two decided on what you want?"

"The special for me," Mack told her.

The woman scribbled down the information,

then looked pointedly at Oren. "What about you, scrawny? Looks like you could use a double-plate special."

From the very first day Oren had walked into the café with Mack, Laverne had teased him mercilessly and Oren was always trying to get her back. Now he playfully pulled a face at her.

"No meat loaf for me, Laverne. Give me a double-meat, loaded burger, fries and a piece of rhubarb pie."

"We don't have rhubarb today," Laverne said. "We only serve it on Tuesdays and Wednesdays."

"Okay. What do you have on Thursdays?" he asked.

"You want the meringue choices or the fruit?"

"Fruit."

The waitress named off a list of pie flavors until Oren held up a hand to halt her.

"Blueberry, that's it," he told her, then gave her a sassy wink. "And for your information I'm not scrawny. If you saw me without any clothes on, you'd know so."

Mack watched the waitress sweep a skeptical gaze up and down Oren's tall frame.

"Not interested," she said blandly. "But those girls at the table across the room probably would be."

Oren's face turned red and Mack couldn't choke back a laugh.

With her pen still poised above her pad, Laverne asked, "Is that all?"

"That's plenty," Mack told her, then continued

to chuckle as the woman turned and headed toward the kitchen.

"Guess I asked for that, didn't I?" Oren muttered.

"Don't try to get ahead of Laverne. It'll never happen. She's been here for years and heard it all. Besides, she picks on you because she likes you."

"I'd hate to hear what she'd have to say if she didn't like me," Oren muttered.

Mack picked up his coffee cup, but only managed to lift it halfway to his mouth when the cell phone inside his shirt pocket began to vibrate.

"An emergency?" Oren asked as Mack pulled out the phone and scanned the screen.

"I don't think so. I wanted to make sure it wasn't the school informing me that Kitty was sick again. Thankfully, it's not the school, so I'll let voice mail deal with the call. Otherwise, I'll not get much of lunch break."

"Yeah. You need to fix the way you operate, Mack. The vet I worked for down in Cedar City let the receptionist deal with all the business calls. Only family or close friends had his personal number."

Mack enjoyed a few sips of coffee before he replied. "You don't need to remind me how we're hurting for help. It would be great if the woman Laverne recommended works out."

Oren didn't reply and Mack glanced over to see he was focused intently on something at the front of the room. In fact, the young man's jaw had dropped to leave his mouth partially gaped.

"Who is *that*?"

The wonderous tone to Oren's question told Mack the object of his attention had to be a woman. "I'm sure I wouldn't know."

"Well, I'd sure like to!"

Curious, Mack gave a cursory glance over his shoulder to see a young, slender woman with short blond hair moving into the maze of dining tables. She looked vaguely familiar and then it dawned on him as to where he'd seen her.

With a wan smile, Mack looked back at Oren. "What a coincidence. We were just talking about receptionists and one walks in."

"You know *her*?"

Mack nodded. "She works the front desk at Pine Valley Clinic. I think her name is Hailey. No, it was Harper…or something like that. I wasn't paying much attention."

He'd been too busy worrying about Kitty and wondering where he was going to find the nerve to face Grace again, Mack thought ruefully.

Oren playfully grabbed one side of his rib cage. "Oh! I just felt an awful pain in my side."

"The blonde doesn't treat patients," Mack pointed out. "She only makes appointments for them."

"Well, in that case I need one." He leaned forward eagerly and snapped his fingers. "Mack, she's the sort of woman you need to hire! Your office would be overrun with male customers."

"Sure! And I'd be spending most of my time chasing my assistant out of the waiting area." Above Oren's shoulder, he spotted Laverne coming their way with a loaded tray of food. "Here comes our lunch. Maybe Laverne can tell you whether Eleanor is a raving beauty."

"Ha! I'm not giving her another chance to make me look like a fool," Oren said.

Years ago, Mack had made a mighty big fool of himself when he'd fallen in love with Grace. But since then he'd learned to never hand over his heart to a woman and, so far, he'd managed to hold fast to the difficult lesson.

Mack grunted. "Women tend to do that to us men, Oren. It's just a fact of life."

Each year on the Monday night before Thanksgiving, the town's business owners provided a free dinner to anyone who wanted to attend. Ever since Grace had returned to Beaver after living a few years in Salt Lake City, she'd always contributed to the charity meal by giving food and helping in the kitchen.

Tonight was no exception. Except that she and Ross were running late as she steered her SUV into the large parking lot located next to the town's civic building. A huge number of vehicles were already taking up the parking slots, forcing Grace to settle for a spot at the far end of the area.

"Gosh, Mom, we're going to have a long walk

from here," Ross said as he unsnapped his seat belt. "Couldn't you get any closer?"

"Sorry, lazy bones," Grace told him. "This is the only space left and it won't hurt you to walk."

He groaned. "Yeah, but we have to carry all this food."

Grace climbed out of the vehicle and hurriedly pulled on a gray trench coat to ward off the cold wind sweeping across the parking lot. "That's right. So hurry and jump out and make yourself useful."

Shrugging on a puffy nylon coat, the boy joined his mother at the back of the SUV. "We must be the last ones here. Do you think they've started eating yet?"

"Probably. But don't worry," she told him as she opened the hatch on the SUV. "There will be plenty to go around. Just remember we're here to help others, not ourselves."

She placed a cardboard box holding a ham into Ross's arms, then picked up a two large plastic shopping bags loaded with bakery goods. After closing the hatch and locking the vehicle, mother and son walked toward the redbrick building.

"I imagine you're going to see some of your classmates here tonight," she told him.

"Bobby said he'd be here tonight. And Trevor said he might get to come. I hope he does," Ross said. "It's more fun when you get to eat with friends."

He glanced curiously up at his mother. "Mom, do you have any friends?"

Grace was accustomed to having Ross ask her all kinds of questions, some of which were a bit weird. But this one brought her up short. "Of course, I have friends, Ross. What makes you ask such a thing?"

"'Cause I never see you with any."

She said, "All the women I work with are my friends. And the people we attend church with are all friends."

"Yeah," Ross said. "But you don't have a friend you go places with or do things together."

Her son had noticed that about her? He was definitely growing up, she thought.

"Hmm. Do you mean like a boyfriend?"

"Sorta something like that," he agreed.

And why had Ross been thinking about this sort of thing? Grace wondered. When he'd been smaller, he had often begged her to get him a father. However, now that he'd gotten older and understood a daddy wasn't something his mother could pluck from a tree, he'd quit asking.

"Ross, I don't want a boyfriend. At least, not right now. I'm too busy being a doctor."

He frowned as though her reasoning didn't make sense. "But, Mom, you're always going to be a doctor."

"Yes. I will always be a doctor," she replied, while thinking she'd already tried being a girlfriend and a wife. Neither had worked out the way she'd planned. Yes, she wished more than anything that Ross had a father, but Bradley had been dead five years now and even before his death, she'd obtained a divorce. No. The only father Ross could hope to have now would be a stepfather and so far she'd not met anyone here.

To Grace's relief, they finished the walk to the building without Ross throwing any more dating questions her way, and by the time they stepped into the busy kitchen he'd turned his mind back to eating.

After turning the food over to a pair of kitchen helpers, Ross asked, "Mom, is it okay if I go out to the dining room?"

"Not yet. Just wait over there by that far wall while I speak to Dorothy about helping with the serving. I'll come tell you."

Ross left to do as she instructed and Grace made her way through the bustling workers until she reached a middle-aged woman with a messy bun and harried smile. Grace didn't know how the woman managed to do it, but every year Dorothy successfully orchestrated this whole event for the townspeople.

"Happy Thanksgiving before Thanksgiving!" she said with a little laugh. She gave Grace a brief hug. "I'm glad you could make our dinner tonight."

"I wouldn't have missed it for anything, Dorothy. And I'm ready to help serve," Grace told her. "Just show me what you want me to do."

The woman shook her head. "Honestly, Grace, we already have more help than we need. People are tripping over each other back here. And you've done more than enough by donating food. You and Ross go on and mingle with the townsfolk. We're almost ready to begin serving."

"Are you sure, Dorothy? I'm more than happy to do my part."

With a laugh of dismay, Dorothy patted Grace's arm. "Oh, my, you're one of the hardest-working persons in Beaver, Grace. And believe me, we all appreciate you. So scram. Go enjoy the meal."

Seeing there was no point in arguing with the woman, Grace thanked her and made her way over to where Ross was impatiently shifting his weight from one cowboy boot to the other.

"Dorothy says I'm not needed," Grace told him. "So let's go out to the dining area, where everyone is gathering. Maybe you'll spot Bobby or Trevor."

"Yay! Let's go!"

At the far end of the room, they passed through a pair of open doors and were suddenly faced with a thick crowd blocking the entryway.

"Gosh, Mom, I think everybody in town is here," Ross commented as he tried to peer around a group of men standing in front of them. "Reckon there will be room for us to sit down?"

Going home and cooking a meal for her and Ross might actually be easier than fighting their way through the crowd, Grace thought. But they were already here and she didn't want Ross to view her as a party pooper. Especially since this event was primarily given for the needy townsfolk.

"We'll see how things are after people start going

through the serving line," she told him. "Right now let's find a quieter spot to stand."

They were slowly working their way along the wall toward an open space at the back of the room, when Grace felt a hand come down on the back of her shoulder.

Expecting to see a coworker, she was stunned when she turned and found herself staring straight into Mack Barlow's face.

"Hello, Grace."

Nearly two weeks had passed since he and Kitty had come to the clinic. She'd not seen or heard from him since. But that hadn't stopped her from thinking about him. To be honest, she'd thought about little else.

"Good evening, Mack."

As she met his gaze, her heart gave one hard thump, then leaped into such a fast pace that the rush of blood caused her ears to roar.

"Hi, Dr. Grace! My tummy is really good now. Are you gonna eat turkey with us?"

Grace's gaze dropped from Mack to Kitty, who was standing at her father's side, clutching a fold on the leg of his jeans. She was wearing a blue velvet dress with a white Peter Pan collar, and a pair of silver cowboy boots with sparkling rhinestones on the shafts. A wide velvet headband the same color as her dress held her dark hair away from her sweet little face. She looked so adorable that bittersweet tears pricked the back of Grace's eyes.

"Hello, Kitty. I'm very happy to hear your tummy is feeling well. But I—I'm not sure if there'll be enough room for all four of us to sit down together."

"I imagine we can find room enough somewhere," Mack said.

Did he want her and Ross to sit with them? More importantly, did she want to spend this evening in his company?

The questions were running through her mind when she felt Ross tugging on her hand to catch her attention.

Taking him by the shoulders, she said, "Ross, this is Mr. Barlow. He's the new veterinarian in town. And, Mack, this is my son, Ross."

"Nice to meet you, Ross." Mack reached down and shook Ross's hand, then urged Kitty to take a step forward. "This is my daughter, Kitty."

The girl gave Ross a long, critical look then she shot her father an inquiring glance. "Is it okay for me to shake Ross's hand, too?"

Mack nodded. "If it's okay with Ross."

The girl held her hand out to Ross and the hearty shake he gave it put a wide, smile on her face.

"My name is Kitty and I'm five," she told Ross. "How old are you?"

"I'm seven," Ross told her. "Do you go to school?"

Kitty gave him a proud nod. "I'm in kindergarten—at Canyon Academy. Do you go to school?"

Ross shot his mother an amused grin before he

answered Kitty's question. "Sure, I do. I go to Canyon Academy, too. I'm in second grade."

Kitty's expression said she was properly impressed. "You must be awful smart."

Ross's face turned a light shade of pink. "I don't know." He cast a doubtful glance at his mother. "Am I, Mom?"

Grace and Mack both laughed.

Clearly amused with his daughter, Mack said, "Kitty admires smartness in a person."

Grace said, "Well, I might have a biased opinion, but I think Ross is smart. He makes good grades."

"I'm gonna make good grades, too," Kitty announced, then directed her next statement to Ross. "I have a horse and a dog. And two cats. Do you have any animals?"

He nodded. "I have a horse. Her name is Penny, 'cause she's red and she's a mare. She stays at my grandpa's ranch. And I have two cats, too. George and Ginger."

Kitty giggled and Grace was a bit surprised that Ross appeared to be totally charmed by the girl's reaction.

"George and Ginger," Kitty repeated. "Those are funny names. I just call my cats *Cat*."

"Why?" Ross asked.

Tilting her head to one side, Kitty contemplated his question. "Because they live in the barn and when I try to play with them they run from me. So I don't think they want names."

Ross stepped closer to Kitty and the children went into a deeper conversation about their cats. While the two of them continued to talk, Grace looked at Mack and smiled.

"Kitty must love animals as much as Ross."

"When we're home on the ranch, I can hardly keep her inside," Mack admitted. "She wants to live at the barn."

"Sounds like she takes after her father. Remember the baby goats you raised on a bottle? You took them on our picnic, just so you wouldn't miss their feeding time. I knew then that you'd be caring for animals the rest of your life."

Mack's gaze met hers and suddenly she was transported back to when the two of them were very young and very much in love. They had spent many days riding and exploring the Broken B and dreaming about making their home on his family ranch. When she thought of those days, she always viewed them through a warm, golden haze of sunshine. Even now, after all these years, it was hard for her to believe he'd wanted their relationship to end. But where Mack was concerned, she'd always been a bit blinded.

A wan smile touched his lips. "Actually, both of those goats are still on the ranch," he told her. "Mildred and Morris are old now, but in good shape for their age."

At least the goats had survived all these years, even if Mack's love for Grace hadn't, she thought.

"Wow. Your father must've taken good care of them."

He shrugged. "Dad made sure they were pampered. Now Kitty loves seeing after them."

As he spoke, his expression shifted subtly and Grace found herself staring at him and wondering. Was that regret she was seeing? Sadness?

No. He'd been talking about goats and nothing else. She needed to quit weighing every expression that crossed his face, each word that rolled out of his mouth.

"I'm sure she does," she said, then, realizing her voice had taken on a husky tone, she cleared her throat and glanced toward the front of the long room. Thankfully, she spotted Dorothy stepping out of the kitchen and ringing the dinner bell.

"Looks like they're going to start serving," Grace announced as the milling crowd began to slowly migrate toward the buffet tables.

Overhearing his mother, Ross exclaimed, "Yay! I'm hungry!"

"Me, too!" Kitty added with eager excitement.

Ross turned to the girl with an all-important question. "Are you going to eat turkey or ham?"

Her little eyebrows pulled together as she contemplated the two choices. "What are you going to eat?" she asked him.

"Ham!"

"Then I'll eat ham, too!" she said happily.

Ross looked hopefully at his mother. "Can we get in line now?"

Grace glanced at Mack. "Are you ready?"

"From the looks of this crowd, better now than later," he agreed.

As the four of them began to head toward the side of the room where a line was already forming, Grace was more than surprised to see Ross reach for Kitty's hand.

"You'd better hang on to me, Kitty," he said to the girl. "Or you might get lost."

Kitty gave him a beaming smile. "I'll hang on real tight," she promised.

While the children moved a few steps in front of their parents, Grace cast a look of amazement at Mack.

"I've never seen him behave this way," she said in a voice too low for Ross to hear. "Does Kitty normally take this quickly to boys?"

He let out a short laugh. "She never takes this quickly to any kid, girl or boy. And that's the biggest smile I've seen on her face since we moved here."

"I'm glad. Hopefully Kitty will get more than a meal out of this evening," Grace said. "She'll get a new friend."

He slanted her a wry smile. "Maybe I'll get more out of this evening, too."

Grace very nearly stumbled. What was he talking about? Spending time with her? No! Her imagination was working far too hard, she thought. She and Mack had been more than friends…once. She'd be silly to think they could ever be more than friends again.

Yet as they maneuvered their way toward the long line of waiting diners, she felt Mack's hand lightly rest against the small of her back. And foolish or not, she realized the contact felt just as good as it had all those years ago.

Don't miss
Rancher to the Rescue *by Stella Bagwell,*
wherever Harlequin® Special Edition
books and ebooks are sold.

www.Harlequin.com